# Riders of the Pony Express

## L. G. Holmes

A Black Horse Western

ROBERT HALE · LONDON

© 1951, 2003 Gordon Landsborough
First hardcover edition 2003

ISBN 0 7090 7349 6

Robert Hale Limited
Clerkenwell House
Clerkenwell Green
London EC1R 0HT

Typeset by
Derek Doyle & Associates, Liverpool.
Printed and bound in Great Britain by
Antony Rowe Limited, Wiltshire

# Riders of the Pony Express

Although it was revolutionary, the Pony Express was not commercially viable carrying mail alone, so a parallel haulage service was introduced. But its established rivals did not welcome the fledgling company and a fierce trade war erupted.

The first act of sabotage was a full-scale night attack, driving a herd of Pony Express oxen to their deaths in a box canyon. But the killing would not stop at only animal life. Jack Irons, Pacific Coast manager of the Pony Express finds himself and his men caught up in a battle to the death with Jud Awker, head of a rival company. Now there is a desperate fight with no holds barred. Can they keep open the trail they had blazed 2,000 miles across the United States?

# CHAPTER ONE

There was a dust-haze stretching for miles back into the desert on this high steppe-land in the heart of Nevada. Fifty miles ahead reared the mighty peaks of the Sierra Nevadas, the last great natural barrier before the Pacific and the fabulous gold wealth of the newly-opened Californian mines. There was glistening white snow on those ragged peaks, though the land below fried in the heat of a late-May sun.

In time the slow-swirling dust-haze parted, to reveal a line of ox-drawn wagons that stretched seemingly to the horizon. It was the mightiest cavalcade that the West had seen since the great Mormon migration of just over a quarter of a century before.

A few men, newcomers to the Far West, had caught up with the slow-moving train and were riding far to one side of it, to keep out of the dust. When they saw the mighty column stretching ahead they grew astonished and rode in closer so that they could conduct a shouted conversation with a perspiring, swearing teamster.

'Where you goin'?' bellowed the prospector, cupping his hands to his mouth to lift his voice above the dejected lowing of the cattle and the harsh grating of iron-tyred wheels on stony soil.

The teamster looked too weary to want a conversation, but growled back, 'Virginie City – an' then 'Frisco.'

The riders looked forward and then back along the column. They saw that the wagons were almost empty, and that astonished them.

'Who owns these wagons?' was the next shouted query.

The teamster sent his whip curling over the backs of his eight patient, plodding beasts. It was a gesture of exasperation, and his voice was wrathful when he answered them. 'We're the Russell, Majors an' Waddell outfit from Kansas, movin' in ter get a share of the haulage 'n Californy. Now what good does that information do yer?'

He was caked red with the desert dust that the oxen kicked up; he was impatient at their slowness, after these months on the trail – he was fed up and in a surly mood, just ready to enjoy a snarling match with a stranger.

The prospector and his companions, tough, unshaven and raggedly dressed, looked mean when they heard his words, but they didn't get quarrelsome. They rode on, marvelling at the length of the column, contenting themselves with a contemptuous, 'You're a nice guy!' to the sullen teamster.

He wasn't the only one. Trekking West in those days when a road was any place where a wheel had rolled before was a gruelling experience. Some of the teamsters wore coloured bandannas over their nostrils and mouths to keep back the bitter red dust;

but even so it was thick in their bushed-up eyebrows, it hung heavy on their lashes, and always it was creeping into their eyes, blinding them with smarting tears of pain.

The prospectors didn't attempt any further conversation. Those huddled, touchy figures up on their wagon seats were too intimidating for that. They rode on, steadily gaining on the leaders.

One was saying, 'Two miles an hour, that's all they do – ef they're lucky. Ten miles a day ef the goin's bad.' When suddenly they stiffened in their saddles, wondering.

A shout had gone up from the leading teamster, a quarter of a mile ahead. It grew louder, as teamster after teamster reared stiffly from his seat, turned and bellowed the news excitedly back.

All in one moment it seemed that the ox drivers had lost their tiredness, had forgotten their sullenness and bad temper, and were as excited as spectators at a Texas rodeo.

The bellowing shouting drew level with them, then passed and went receding into the four miles distance where the last wagon rolled. Every teamster was standing on his seat now, staring ahead through the dust haze, and cursing it because their vision was restricted.

One of the prospectors called to his companions, 'Did you get that?'

The others shouted above the din of trundling wheels, 'Nope, what's bitin' 'em?'

Their companion had got the message, however, and he seemed bitten, too. He was standing in his stirrups, pointing ahead and shouting.

They saw, far ahead, a tiny cloud of dust, advancing at a prodigious rate. Then they began to discern a black figure that was in advance of the dust and the cause of it – a black, moving object that swayed and rose and fell and was sometimes lost to sight below an undulation in the rough, scrub desert.

Suddenly, all at once, it seemed, that black object became discernible as a horse and rider – but a horse and rider travelling at a speed they'd never known before. Then the prospectors understood, and they rose in their stirrups and cheered like mad.

The rider came on with a rush, lying so flat along the neck of his horse that they could scarcely see him. And his horse – a mighty black stallion that was the picture of speed and power . . . its feet seemed not to touch the ground, so lightly did it run, so beautifully balanced was its stride; it skimmed the track as if no effort was being put into the motion, and yet it was travelling at an astonishing pace.

Within minutes the horse and rider were abreast of the leading wagon; then it came flashing down the long line, to the accompaniment of frenzied cheering from the teamsters, holding back on their reins now to stop the wagons and so not miss a second of this moment.

A rattle of hoofs, a swirl of dust that enveloped the prospectors, and the rider was away, racing down the trail towards Austin.

The teamsters had jumped down from their seats and were standing out from the track, watching after the rider. They were cheerful and jubilant, suddenly in the best of tempers.

One hoary ruffian bellowed delightedly to the

prospectors, "Ain't that somethin' ter see? Have you ever seen anythin' like that in your born days?"

And the marvelling prospectors admitted they hadn't.

"The Pony Express," that old ruffian said proudly. And then, to crown his happiness, he was able to boast – "*Our* Pony Express!"

But the prospectors didn't know what he was talking about. Didn't know that the company of Russell, Majors and Waddell, the big Middle West freight contractors, were the owners of this mail experiment that had thrilled the great new American continent.

It had made its first run little more than a month before, on April 3rd, 1860. Every day now – and every night, too – eighty riders were in constant motion over a course that stretched from the rail-head at St Joseph in Missouri to Sacramento in California. Some rocketed westward, while others shuttled eastwards in the longest relay race the world had ever known, along a course that stretched nineteen hundred miles.

Nineteen hundred miles ... but not nineteen hundred easy miles. It ran through Kansas and Nebraska, along the Platte with its formidable, hostile Sioux and other Indian tribes, over the mighty Rocky Mountains and across the inferno of the Utah deserts. It was gruelling, killing work, but every day now the horses ran and the mails were carried through.

Nineteen hundred miles – and rarely did it take longer than nine days to get the precious mails delivered from the railhead to the Pacific coast or

9

vice versa.

They were proud of the experiment, here in the West. For years they had tried to establish a service which could bring mails through in a matter of days instead of months by clipper round the Horn. Now that the big freight haulage company had instituted the Pony Express it had become the most popular, the most talked-about experiment in the New World.

In fact, the carrying of mails had become second in the minds of most men. It was the drama behind the delivery of every letter that gripped their imaginations. And besides, too, it was like having a race meeting almost every day – everywhere along the route men had bets as to the time of the arrival of the mail at some rest station or other. The Pony Express had certainly written a page in the history of the West, even in its short life to date.

An hour after the pony rider had gone thundering eastwards, and the reluctant, day-dreaming teamsters had mounted their own, slow-going wagons – every man a romantic Pony Express rider for the moment – the order was given to circle up for the night.

Because of the recent unrest among the Nevada Indians, no risks were taken, and the site for the night's halt was in the open away from the foothills, with only sparse grass and withered sage brush to provide any sort of cover for an enemy.

But because of the length of the column, because it would have taken at least two hours before the last crawling vehicle could come up with the circle, two camps were made about three miles apart across the level desert.

Dusk came, and with it dozens of leaping fires glowed out across the plain, advertising the presence of the two great camps. And there were eyes to see, and minds to act upon the information.

Around ten o'clock that starry, moonless night, the two camps were asleep except for the out-riders who circled the wagon rings and the herds of resting oxen that were grouped about them.

The men were tired, because this was first watch after a wearying day on the hot desert, but they were alert enough.

Suddenly, from the camp nearest Virginia City, a sharp cry rang out. Other riders came galloping round to see the cause of the disturbance. Three men converged upon a fourth, stationary horseman.

One called, 'That you, Luke? What made you shout?'

Luke was peering into the darkness, his rifle ready to fire. He growled back, 'I figger thar's someone skulkin' out thar in the sage. I saw somethin' move; I shouted, an' whoever it was slipped away.'

The four horsemen peered into the night's blackness. They felt jumpy, feeling they could be seen without being able to see. It wasn't a good feeling.

One of them opined, hoarsely, 'Injuns!' No one argued with him. If anyone was out there in the sagebrush it seemed logical to assume they were red men.

Nothing stirred. Only a low, depressed moan from a weary ox broke the silence of the Nevada night. In time they grew tired of sitting there, listening, and one of the horsemen pulled round and growled, 'Mebbe there was no one, Luke. Mebbe your eyes

11

made things up for you.'

He didn't say it with any offensive meaning, because he knew too well the tricks a man's eyes got up to in this desert darkness, especially after a trying day in the sun and without rest for nearly eighteen hours.

Luke said, 'Mebbe.' He wasn't so sure himself. He growled, 'But I could have sworn it . . . Mebbe you'd better git back, though, in case anythin' starts over the other side.'

They turned their horses at that and split up, leaving Luke to watch with suspicious unease the blackness about him. His eyes darted everywhere, any sleep there might have been in them earlier dissipated now by thoughts of possible danger. The worst of it was that every bush looked like a lurking form, every depression in the desert could hold someone hostile who would be hidden even at five yards' distance.

He clucked his tongue at his horse and walked it along in front of the cud-chewing oxen, down on their stomachs. About ten strides, that horse went.

Then something moved from behind a bush that Luke had just passed; a black form lifted and silently stalked the slow-moving rider. Luke felt something spring over the horse's haunches behind him, felt a bony, bare forearm crook round his throat, tightening. He tried to shout, but only a harsh gurgling sound rose from his throat; he struggled frantically to free himself, but managed only to pull them both off the horse.

They crashed to the ground, the horse rearing and running away. The fall didn't break that hold.

After a very short interval Luke stopped struggling. Then the shadow lifted from off his back and stood like a man listening.

No one had heard the few sounds that had betrayed their struggle. The camp was undisturbed.

A sound came to the lips of the assailant. It was the noise of the nightjar, soft but insistent, carrying even to the ears of the other riders around the circle, but seeming to them only another harmless night sound.

Within seconds more dark figures had appeared, only this time they were mounted on horses that wore cloths around their jaws to prevent them from whinnying betrayingly. The horsemen silently headed for the oxen. There must have been a dozen of them.

A gun suddenly crackled off – and the camp came rudely out of its slumbers. Another gun blasted, puncturing the night's blackness with scarlet fire, and then a fusillade of gun-fire shattered any lingering rays of optimism that anyone could hold.

Men came tumbling from their blankets, reaching for guns and kicking on their boots. Everywhere men were calling to each other, shouting queries, and it was confusing. Then the trail boss roared for them to shut their heads and come towards him.

Out there in the blackness beyond the wagon circle it seemed as though a battle was raging. They could hear wild whooping voices along with the roar of guns, and at once the cry went up from the wagoners – 'Injuns! It's an Injun attack!'

A new sound was growing in volume, however, that began to drown the noise of men's whooping voices and the banging of Colts and the cracking of rifles. It was the voice of fear-crazed oxen.

It began with a few bellows, then rose to a mighty, frenzied roar. Then the earth began to shake as heavy hoofs bit into the ground as the oxen started to gallop frantically away from the frightening noises that had come to disturb their rest.

The wagonmaster got into something of a panic himself. He cursed and raved, and then roared, 'Them Injuns is stampedin' the cattle. Marty, take a dozen men an' git out an' see what you c'n do!'

But he was too wise to take any more men from the circle of defenders. If this was an Indian attack, they had better stick behind their defences if they wished to remain alive.

Marty and his hastily-picked men grabbed horses and rode out. The trouble was that in that blackness no one knew what was happening, and they had to be guided by sound rather than sight. It had the one advantage of being as much cover for the little band of riders under Marty as it was for the attackers, and old Marty, who had fought his first Indian fifty years before, wasn't slow in pointing that out to the more reluctant of his men.

They rode straight across to where the oxen were in stampede. There was still a lot of shooting, but the dust was lifting and further hiding events from sight.

All Marty had learned after ten minutes was that their precious draught oxen were in mad stampede through the darkness, heading for the broken country that lay in their path towards Virginia City. Behind the oxen rode the whooping, gun-firing attackers.

He sent a messenger racing back to the camp to say, 'Thar's a party of Injuns stampedin' the cattle. Thar ain't much we c'n do in the dark, but we'll try'n foller 'em.'

Long before dawn, however, Marty had given up the chase and had settled down in the sagebrush with his men to wait for daylight. In that darkness they just ran the risk of killing themselves and their horses if they tried to go at any pace whatever, and by now the oxen had scattered and were running separately or in very small groups and it was hopeless to try to round them up.

The attackers had faded away, too, very soon after the mad stampede had begun. All at once the firing had stopped and the shouting had died, and there were no dim forms careering at crazy speed on horseback in the darkness of the night.

It was an apprehensive camp that saw the first light from the east that morning, and they looked out upon a scene of desolation and disaster.

Their herd of draught oxen had gone – all but a few brown forms lying in the sagebrush where the stampede had taken its course. The wagonmaster, a Leavenworth man named Thompson, scanned the plain for Indians, decided there weren't any, and immediately sent his men out to follow the oxen.

All along the way they found dead or injured beasts – valuable animals that had broken limbs in holes in the dark and gone down and been trampled on by their kind. The injured were shot out of hand, because there would be no time for surgery on this trek to California.

They found Luke in the sagebrush. He wasn't

dead, but he had been knocked about, while he was unconscious, by the charging animals. Four men dismounted and carried their companion back to the camp.

Then they found two more of their men, one of them a night rider, the other a man who had ridden out with Marty. Both had been shot. It looked as though they had run into their assailants and had lost a fight in the dark.

Sometime later Wagonmaster Thompson ran into Marty. Marty had rounded up a few of the runaways, but his face was long as they joined him. He told them these were all the beasts that had come through the night alive.

Thompson looked thunderstruck. He looked at the grizzled old man and demanded, 'Marty, what'n heck are you sayin'? Whar's all the other beasts?'

Marty pointed back along behind him, where buzzards were already circling on the rim of the desert horizon. He growled, 'Them beasts is thar, Tommy, an' you'll never slip another collar over their necks. Thar's a canyon – only a small affair, 'bout forty yards wide. It's not deep, either – but jest deep enough fer a cow ter break its blamed neck ef it goes tumblin' down from the top. Like ours did in the darkness last night.'

It was a stunning, overwhelming loss. The company had begun this expensive Pony Express service so as to extend their interests into California. They had planned to open up as freight haulers over the Nevadas, so as to cover their operations, and here in one night they had lost a good part of their precious draught animals.

They herded their beasts back to camp and to the breakfast that had been prepared in their absence. Thompson said, 'We'll have ter stay here a while. Them oxen are leg-weary an' will have ter be rested up; then we'll have ter hitch four up an' bring the wagons in that way.'

Four instead of the more usual eight or twelve beasts to a wagon didn't promise a fast run in to Virginia City even when they did get going, and the impatient men were depressed at the thought of the crawl over the next leg of their journey.

Thompson despatched a fast rider ahead, to tell the Pacific Coast manager about the affair. 'Tell him we'll be late arrivin' on account of some blamed Injuns that ran off with our beasts an' got a lot killed.'

'Injuns?' Old Marty heard him and looked up sharply. Thompson continued with his message, his face scowling because he was wagonmaster and he felt the disgrace of his position keenly.

'Tell him I'll bring the wagons in, but until we get more beasts we'll not be able to operate over the Sierras like the company want. We lost over four hundred cattle in that stampede last night, tell him, an' I don't know where he's gonna get replacements this side of the continent.'

The rider pulled away, and soon was a tiny dust cloud ascending into the foothills. Then someone shouted that a band of horsemen were riding in from the direction of the other camp.

Thompson growled, 'It's about time, too.' He was in a bad temper and sought to lay blame wherever he could.

His assistant, Shep Clayton, was with the party. Thompson shouted, 'Didn't you hear the hullabuloo last night?'

Clayton reined and looked down at his angry face. He was a calm young man and didn't get excited. He drawled, 'Sure I heard it. Sure we all heard it. Reckon they heard the noise back in Salt Lake City.'

Thompson bristled at the tone. He was missing his night's rest now and his temper roughened his tongue.

'Why'n hell didn't you come out ter help us, then?'

Clayton rapped back, 'Why didn't you send over fer help?'

'We was too damn' busy, that's why.' Thompson glared angrily.

So Clayton said, 'An' that's my answer, too.'

The Thompson men came crowding round in astonishment at that. 'What?' cried the wagonmaster. 'Did you run into trouble?'

'We sure did. When we heard the commotion over here we got together an' talked about it. We opined there was a big force of Injuns attackin' you, an' we expected maybe they'd come an' attack us soon. But they didn't, so a dozen of us thought ter ride through an' give you a hand, leavin' the rest ter keep guard over the wagons.'

Thompson had lost his bad temper and nodded approval of the caution.

'Wal, we'd just rid out from the wagons, an' the night was as black as ink, when we ran into trouble. Someone opened up with rifles from the darkness an' drove us back. We didn't have anyone killed, but five of my men stopped lead somewhere or other. So we rode back to our camp an' kept watch all night fer an attack that never came.'

He took off his soiled, broad-brimmed hat and said, thoughtfully, 'I don't reckon there was anythin' else we c'd do, was there, Tommy? I mean – wal, that black night sure had us licked. There wasn't a thing we dare do ter help you.'

Thompson agreed with him, his temper gone. 'Sure, Shep, that's all right. Sorry I talked rough at you.' He sighed, then sought desperately to find a consoling feature about the night's work. 'Anyway, it's good ter know you didn't suffer any losses yourself.'

'Only five men punctured,' Clayton said drily.

'Men? Thar's plenty men in these parts,' Thompson said impatiently. 'But you can't get cattle to replace what you've lost, not easily.'

They talked awhile, then Clayton rode off to bring his wagons up and make one big camp for the night at the scene of the stampede.

Late that afternoon a lone rider came hurrying in on a big, black stallion. At first they thought it might be a pony rider, because he came in fast, but then they saw he was too big for the job and they guessed who it was.

'Jack Irons,' exclaimed Thompson, walking out to meet him.

'Iron Jack,' said his men, giving him the name that had become attached to him as a Ranger operating against the Mexicans in the Border wars. He had a reputation in the West, this big, lean cattleman turned agent for the big haulage company – for most, a good reputation.

19

But among those two hundred teamsters and out-riders were a few Kansas men with long memories, and they thought of the bills that had been tacked to tavern doors and tree trunks many a year back – bills which said, 'Wanted for Murder, Jack Irons.'

There was a reward out now amounting to five hundred dollars to any man who could bring Jack Irons back into the State of Kansas, dead or alive.

And some of those men there had thoughts about trying it.

# CHAPTER TWO

Irons swung down. He had travelled far and fast and his big horse was swaying with exhaustion as he came stiffly out of the creaking saddle. He had a good face, bronzed as deep as an Indian's from a life outdoors, grey-eyed and intelligent. There wasn't the hardness in it that was to be seen on so many men's faces, here in the rough-and-tumble pioneering West, yet it wasn't weak or soft. It was very much a man's face . . .

Irons shook hands with the wagonmaster, whom he had never met before. He drawled, in a voice that had started in Kansas but had acquired the slow-laziness of Texas in more recent years, 'Looks like you hit trouble – plenty trouble, Thompson.'

'We sure did.' The wagonmaster's face was grim. 'I'd like to get them destructive Injuns on the foresight o' my gun, that's all I c'n say, Jack.'

'You reckon Injuns was the cause of the trouble?' Irons had been using his eyes as he rode in, and he hadn't missed that canyon with its burden of dead oxen.

Thompson shrugged. 'Who else would do a thing

21

like start a stampede but a blamed redskin?' His eyes sought out Marty, the old Indian fighter. 'Marty here says it's the queerest Injun attack he's ever known, but he can't think who else could have done it if not Injuns.'

Iron Jack looked at the grizzled old frontiersman. 'You figger this ain't Injun warfare?'

Marty spat. 'I never knew an Injun that was content just ter pile up a lot o' cattle an' not try'n make somethin' outa the deal fer himself.'

Iron Jack said, 'Mebbe they drove off a few cows in the mix-up.'

Marty retorted, 'Mebbe – but they didn't. I've bin out circlin' fer tracks all day, an' them Injuns didn't drive off any bunch o' oxen last night.' To confirm it, he added, 'It was so dark, they couldn't have managed it, anyway.'

Big Jack Irons went right up to the Indian fighter then and confronted him. 'You've got somethin' on your mind, Marty,' he said softly. 'C'mon, old timer, speak out. Mebbe it's gonna help us all a lot.'

But Marty could only shrug helplessly and say, 'Aw, Jack, mebbe I'm just bein' an old fool. Mebbe this was Injun work after all.' He hesitated, then came out with it, leaning back against the wide-tyred wheel of a freight wagon.

'Them Injuns was usin' Colts last night – usin' 'em a lot. I figger every blamed redskin had his hand on a Colt, an' – wal, a Colt ain't an Injun weapon at all.'

'Nope.' Iron Jack agreed with him abruptly, and there was a sudden growl from the men crowding round to hear. 'Injuns like rifles, because rifles c'n shoot game an' they live by what they c'n kill. But a Colt's fer killin' men, an' so far not many's got into the hands of Injuns.'

Someone said, 'The Injuns don't like Colts. They don't have much ammunition, so they trade fer rifles always, not pistols.'

The men began to argue amongst themselves, but in general they agreed with Marty.

Marty answered a doubt in Iron Jack's mind before it was spoken. 'OK, Jack, I know what's on your tongue. You think mebbe I can't tell the sound of a Colt from a rifle in the dark, but I tell yer I can, an' I figger most men who were with me last night know the difference.'

There was assent from his followers of the night before. They'd got close to the shooting, and now they all remembered that most of it had been Colt fire. Iron Jack accepted the evidence.

'Looks like this wasn't Injun work, then.' His eyes narrowed. 'But ef it weren't Injun work, whose was it?'

And that was baffling. What men were willing to risk their lives in a sudden raid on a big camp, merely for the pleasure of piling up a lot of valuable cattle in a canyon?

It was baffling. Then someone on the outskirts of their little crowd called, 'Hey, fellars, we got visitors!'

They had. A group of Indians was riding slowly towards them, about eight in number. They weren't elegantly dressed; they looked as drab and nondescript as this sagebrush desert in which they lived.

The suspicious, hostile white men saw Indians wearing old hats and clothing cast off by pioneers along the Californian trail, and they were not impressed, and rough, rude remarks greeted the party as they came to a halt a few yards away.

Iron Jack and the wagonmaster pushed their way out to greet the Indians. The redmen held up their hands, palms facing the white men, to denote their peaceful intentions, and the wagonmaster lifted his hand in return in a careless salute.

'What do you want?' he growled. He wasn't convinced that last night's work wasn't the doings of these desert Indians, and his face showed his hostility to the newcomers.

'Redman come in peace,' grunted the spokesman for the Indians. 'Redman him good man and show him good. Him bring hurt white man for white man's medicine.'

With that speech the Indians became suddenly eager. They parted and a horse was kicked forward. Lying belly down across its back, supported by a young Indian boy rider, was the limp form of a white man.

The wagonmaster grunted, 'Looks like they've picked up some poor devil off the trail, an' figger they'll get a reward fer bringin' him in.'

He walked forward with Iron Jack to look at the man. He lifted the man's head and saw the closed eyes and sagging mouth and knew he was unconscious.

'OK, get him off,' Thompson shouted to his men. Then the Indians began to clamour for food because of their help to the white man. They called that there was little to eat nowadays because the white man in his trek westward had scared all the game away or blasted it out of existence with his long gun.

Thompson nodded to one of his men. 'Get 'em some food.' He spoke grudgingly; he felt that maybe he was being a fool, that he was giving food to the very rascals who had cost his company so much. He didn't like the thought, but he was a fair man at heart, when he wasn't in a temper, and he recognized that it was worth a bit of food to keep the Indians on good terms with the white man.

The Indians went away in high spirits, to receive some flour that was full of weevil, but they didn't mind that, and some dried buffalo meat that looked unappetising but would make fine food when it was cooked. They were told they could also help themselves to the dead oxen on the plain, and that delighted them.

They were about to ride away when Iron Jack called to them to come across to him. He'd been looking at the injured man.

He was white, all right, but in a very bad way. He'd been shot at close range in the neck and had lost a lot of blood. Iron Jack didn't think he'd recover; being brought in slung across a pony like that couldn't have helped him.

The Pacific Coast boss demanded, 'How come you found white man like this?'

The Indian, thinking to get further gifts, was voluble in his explanation. 'This mornin' redman him find white man fallen off his horse along trail. Him losin' blood. Him die plenty quick, but redman stop him blood. We bringum white man's camp when him no get better. Injun him no like wounded white man in lodge. Him make plenty trouble for redman.'

25

'Sure.' Iron Jack nodded. If white men had got to know that a wounded paleface was in an Indian camp they would naturally have assumed that the redman was responsible for his injuries and it could have gone hard for the poor desert Indians.

He felt the wagonmaster, Thompson, bristling by his side. He turned. The shorter, older man's face was black with suspicion now.

'How did you know we were campin' out this way?' Thompson suddenly demanded. Iron Jack knew what he was thinking – logically the Indians should have carried the injured man the opposite way, towards the more thickly populated area around Virginia City.

The Indian's answer satisfied Jack Irons, anyway. 'Redman him see white man's camp easy. Redman him have village in hills, see plenty far across prairie.' His hand waved towards the hill country to the west of them.

Iron Jack said, 'That seems reasonable enough, Thompson. I figger these Injuns are tellin' the truth.'

Old Marty came forward, rubbing his bristly chin. He cocked an eye towards Iron Jack and said, 'I figger more'n that. Me, I got an idea this fellar's one of the gang that druv off our cattle last night.'

Everyone straightened at that, trying to accept this theory. Old Marty kept on talking, sure of himself now. 'I never did feel it was Injuns did that stampedin' last night. Now I reckon fer sure it was white men's work – an' this fellar's one of the gang. Looks like he stopped some lead in that bit of fightin' in the dark last night – mebbe he couldn't keep up with the other *hombres* an' fell outa his saddle up along the trail. Yeah, Jack, I reckon a gang did that last night, mebbe a bunch o' renegades or outlaws.'

They all eyed the old man, and then Thompson asked an irritable question. 'OK, Marty. Then you tell me what'n hell good it did 'em, ter stampede our oxen as they did?'

He was too exasperated, too full of dismay that such a disaster should occur to any wagon train that he was leading, to stand and listen to Marty's reply. He went back to the wagons, to brood on the loss and to think savagely of the Indians he felt responsible for it.

He couldn't accept Marty's theory; it just didn't hang. White men, he thought cynically, never did anything unless they got a reward for doing it. All right, what reward could white men get out of driving valuable oxen into a canyon?

Now the redman, full of bitterness towards the white invader of his hunting grounds, could be expected to do vindictive things, for no other reason than that the white man wouldn't like them.

The group split up, a few men carrying the wounded man in to be looked after with their other casualties. But the big boss, Iron Jack, stayed where he was, and in the end he was left only with Marty.

Marty chewed stolidly on his plug, and waited for Iron Jack to speak. The day was dying and the westering sun tinged the distant snowy Sierras with a glowing red light. Away from their camp, the vast desert was empty of people or animals that they could see.

Iron Jack spoke at length. ' I reckon I figger like you do, Marty. Reckon this ain't Injun work, in spite of what Thompson thinks.'

Marty grunted and spat, and then said, ' 'Bout time someone got ter figgerin' the way I see it.' He spat again. He was a shrivelled old man, but as hardy as the sagebrush all around him. 'You know, Jack, I figger that ain't the last of 'em, whoever they are. Me, I'm opinin' they'll come agen tonight.'

Iron Jack looked around at the long shadows and asked, 'What makes you think so, Marty?'

'Because it don't make sense ef they don't,' Marty shot back. 'Look, Jack, thar's only one reason fer last night's little fireworks – that was ter kill them draught animals.'

Big Jack Irons nodded.

'OK. Wal, look, Jack, all our beasts are together tonight, right in the same position whar they c'n be stampeded ter death into that canyon. Last night I reckon the second camp was either too far away fer 'em, or attackin' two camps at once was just a bit too much for 'em. They attacked this one, the nearest to the canyon, leavin' a few men to see that no one came ridin' out ter help from the second camp along the trail.'

'You figger this has all been nicely planned? Whoever did it had gone over this ground an' seen the possibilities of that canyon right ahead of here?'

'Sure. I figger mebbe they've bin waitin' fer us to come a-crawlin' up fer days – jest waitin' fer a moon-less night . . . an' most nights are without moon fer some hours ef not for all the night.'

So Iron Jack asked the obvious question. 'You got

any ideas about who did it – an' why, Marty?'

The old man shook his head. 'Nope, I ain't got no idea who did it, but I reckon I'm beginnin' ter see why.'

Iron Jack said, softly, 'You figger some Californian haulage contractor doesn't like the idea of the powerful Russell, Majors and Waddell outfit musclin' in on their territory?'

Marty stopped chewing. 'You got that idea, too?'

Iron Jack turned away and began to walk into the wagon ring. 'Yeah, that's how I figgered things right from the moment I saw them cattle piled up in the gulch. More, Marty, I got an idea who's back of this to-do.'

Marty's toothless mouth began to ask questions. Iron Jack reckoned he was pretty safe for confidences, a sound servant of the company, and answered them briefly.

'There's a fellar I know in San Francisco called Jud Awker. He's got the biggest freightin' outfit on this side of the continent, an' he's makin' a pile, now that gold an' silver has bin discovered this side of the Sierras. He doesn't like competition, an' he's pretty ruthless, I c'n tell you. I've met him a few times, an' I figger that little no-good bad-tempered man sure is the nigger in this woodpile, ef anyone is.'

Marty said, 'Wal, Jack, you know him; I don't. But it sounds like it could be that way. It makes sense.'

Iron Jack said, grimly, 'So does your idea that there might be another attack tonight to drive more cattle into the canyon. I'm goin' ter talk things over with Thompson, an' I want you along, old timer.'

He strode away, anxiously looking at the darkening sky above him. Fires were blazing again, and the evening meal was well in preparation. Someone called to him to get food, but though he needed it after that long day in the saddle, he postponed refreshment for a while.

Thompson was sitting against the wheel of a stores wagon. He shouted for coffee to be brought over for Iron Jack when he saw the big boss striding towards him.

Irons took it gratefully, squatting on his heels. He shoved back his hat and spoke straight. 'Tommy, I don't figger that was an Injun attack at all. Anyway, that doesn't matter. What does matter is that Marty here's uneasy – he thinks we're right in a position ter lose the rest of our cattle tonight.'

'Hell, another raid?' Thompson choked at the thought of it.

'Mebbe he's wrong, Tommy,' Iron Jack continued earnestly, 'but I don't reckon we'll run any risks.'

'Nope.' Thompson was too good a wagonmaster to insist on his theories when there was a possibility of danger to the property entrusted to him. He said, 'What's in your mind, Jack?'

So Iron Jack told him. 'Make the circle bigger – you've got plenty wagons. But lock 'em – fasten 'em so they make a solid corral that cattle can't get out of.'

'I see. Tonight the cattle are on the inside of the ring, while we sleep outside?'

'That's the way I figger it. Only tonight we won't sleep much,' Iron Jack said grimly. 'Tonight there'll be no fires to mark our position, an' show us up agen the flames. Tonight we'll be alongside our rifles, under the wagons, an' ef we hear a thing . . . .'

He didn't need to finish his sentence. The others nodded; they approved of the plan.

The men were shouted together, and they came walking up from their fires, still eating their evening meal. They had over two hundred men – a veritable army, but largely ineffective against alert attackers approaching under cover of a near-black night.

Thompson pulled himself into an empty wagon and shouted out details of the big boss's plan, and the men growled back assent to it. They were mean and vicious, after their disturbed night, and were prepared to deal toughly with those responsible for it.

The big outfit swung into life. Men went to their horses and mounted them and rode to round up the placid, munching oxen, while others manhandled the wagons into position and fastened them so that the ring couldn't easily be broken through. It wasn't hard work, moving most of those wagons, because they were empty on this westward migration.

Big Iron Jack stood with Thompson and Shep Clayton, the wagonmaster's young but dependable assistant, and they watched the depleted herd come lowing in through a gap left in the circle to receive the oxen. By the time they were in, it was nearly dark.

Thompson turned to the big boss and rasped, 'That satisfy you Jack?'

'Nearly.' Iron Jack remembered now his hunger, and they walked across to where some food was being dished out. While he was eating, Thompson asked, 'You figgerin' out some other plan?'

'Sure.' Iron Jack gulped as the hot beans went down. 'I don't aim ter let any gang attack our outfit without tryin' ter attack 'em back. But you've got ter know your enemy afore you c'n hit him. So tonight I aim to sit down in that sagebrush an' try'n find out who's back of this attack. I've got my ideas, but that ain't enough. I want proof.' His face went hard and grim, and his brown capable hands smote suddenly together in a gesture of fury and frustration. 'An' ef it's the outfit I think it is, we'll put up the biggest fight the West's seen since the Nevada Indians went under.'

Thompson stared over his coffee admiringly. Evidently the reputation of this ex-Border fighter wasn't misplaced.

He said, 'You're gonna sit over there in the dark all by yourself?' Iron Jack wrapped himself round a lump of pork and nodded. 'But ef we hear anythin', we open fire. How about you then?'

Iron Jack said, carelessly, 'I take my chances. Ef you hear anythin', let 'em have it. I'll be down out of sight, you bet.' His grin inspired confidence; this man wasn't one to enter into any foolhardy schemes, they could see.

Thompson looked at Shep and shook his head. 'All I c'n say is, we're blamed lucky to have you with us, Jack. Lucky fer us they found you so near.'

The big boss laughed off the compliment, not wanting flattery. 'It sure was lucky I rode into Virginie City yesterday. Mostly I stay in the mountains, around Carson City.'

'You came to meet us?'

'Partly,' Iron Jack admitted, but he didn't tell them the other part. He was expecting a stage coach in from Salt Lake City any day now, and there was someone on that coach he badly wanted to see again.

It was a girl whom he had met on the trail not long ago. She had returned to Kansas, and he had thought her lost to him; but the ailing mother she had gone to nurse had died suddenly and now the disconsolate girl was heading back West again.

She was going through to an uncle in San Francisco, but she had written to say that she wanted to see Jack Irons . . . and Jack Irons wanted to see bonny Ann Caudry more than he'd ever wanted to see anyone in his life before.

Darkness came quickly after the sun had sunk below the western Sierras. Thompson went stamping around the wagon circle, shouting for the fires to be put out, and the men to get under the wagons with their guns. He said that half the men could sleep where they lay, but the other half must maintain a constant watch. Any sound from out on the prairie was to be interpreted as hostile, and the men could open fire with everything they had got. The prospect pleased the men, fretting at the inactivity of the day in the desert, and they got down under the wagons without argument.

When Iron Jack saw the last fire go out, and the darkness plummet swiftly upon them, he said good-bye to the wagonmaster and Shep Clayton, and walked out into the night.

He walked westward along the trail. He figured that if the gang returned again that night they would most likely come in from the direction of

Virginia City, for the fact that the unconscious man had been found in that direction suggested that they had come from the town.

He sat down in the sagebrush alongside the track when he was about a mile out from the camp. There was not a sound to be heard except the stir of wind in the scented sagebrush and the creak of some night-prowling insect in the dry stalks.

The big boss lay down, relaxing gratefully because he was tired after his hard day in the saddle. He could have slept easily, there, under the velvety Nevada sky, with its irregular pattern of stars and the beginnings of a thin slice of moon just starting to show over the horizon. But he held off the sleep that his weary body demanded. Tonight there might be work for him to do.

He seemed to lie there for hours, and in time doubt grew in his mind. He began to think that his hunch about the gang returning to try to damage more of the oxen was very much uninspired. In the darkness he gave a wry grin – there'd be some coarse remarks from the teamsters next morning if nothing happened.

But something did happen. Suddenly he heard the clink of harness metal, then the soft plod-plod of slow-walking horses in the darkness. He rolled on to his elbow, listening intently. A fair-sized body of horsemen was approaching.

They seemed to halt for a while a couple of hundred yards away from him – two hundred yards, but in the still quiet of that desert night the low murmur of their conversation was audible to Iron Jack's intent ears.

After some minutes they came walking slowly along the trail again. Iron Jack crouched in the sage-brush as they drew level with him. He got the smell of sweaty horseflesh, heard a man curse in bad temper under his breath, and saw them as vague black silhouettes that came to obscure the stars.

When they had passed he came quietly to his feet and high-stepped it over the bushes on to the open trail and walked cautiously in their tracks.

He felt he was pretty safe. Any slight noise his boots made would be drowned by the creaking of harness leather, and the muffled tread of hoofs in dust. They wouldn't see him in that darkness, either – not before he saw them, he thought. All the same he had his Colt in his hand as he came following softly in their tread.

They halted again, and he nearly ran on to a horse before he realized it – the night was as black as all that. This time Iron Jack was close enough to hear what was being said.

Someone growled, uneasily, 'They're on to us, I tell yer. Else why would they do without fires?'

Another voice cursed him softly for being chicken-livered, and said, reasonably, 'They figger fires'd help Injuns to spot 'em, so they're sleepin' without. They don't want another raid, that's all.'

Still another voice chimed in, and this time it was harsh and rasping, and sound of it made Iron Jack prick up his ears. He'd heard that voice before. Most people on the Pacific Coast had heard that bullying, argumentative voice. Iron Jack was ready to swear that the owner was Jud Awker, the ruthless owner of the biggest freight concern in the West. He'd met

Awker before, had fought against him in order to establish the Pony Express. For Awker had seen in the express overland mail service the thin end of the wedge, the coming of the powerful Kansas freighting interests that would set up in competition with his own outfit; and he had fought hard to ruin the enterprise from the start.

Now it seemed that Awker had turned his attentions to meet the more direct threat of the freight wagons themselves. If he could destroy these draught oxen, he could, probably for some considerable time, retard the entry of Russell, Majors and Waddell into competition with his own big company.

Awker snarled, 'They're gonna get another raid, so no one get ter thinkin' anythin' else, see! They're out there – we saw their camp from the hills. Sittin' without fires won't help 'em. Lope – you'n Flathead get off your hosses an' do a bit o' scoutin' like last night. Find where them cattle is an' see ef we c'n drive 'em into that canyon like we did them others.'

'Ef we can't, boss?' The way the man spoke, Iron Jack figured he was either Indian or a 'breed.

'Ef we can't, we're gonna sit out here in the darkness an' shoot lead into them cattle. By the time we run outa ammunition we'll have damaged a lot of blamed Kansas cows.'

Hearing that brutal, jarring voice, Iron Jack's Colt lifted involuntarily in the darkness, and trained in the direction of the speaker. Then he lowered it. That was no good, taking a pot shot at his enemy in the dark. That would only bring the gang's attentions on him, and wouldn't help the outfit circled up three-quarters of a mile away.

Awker gave an order to dismount and lie up until the return of his scouts, and big Jack Irons went low down in the sagebrush so that his form didn't stand out revealed against the starry night sky. The moon was too low on the horizon to be of any help to him just then, but after a while he found that he could count the horses and it seemed there were fifteen to twenty men in the party.

That didn't sound much, against their own two-hundred-odd burly teamsters and out-riders, but the advantage would be with the attackers who could move at will in the darkness while the freight haulers had to lie up in a compact bunch to defend the company's property.

About half an hour later he heard the scouts return. They gave a pretty good account of the situation, and it made Jud Awker swear. He and his men discussed the situation for a while, and then decided on a plan.

Four men would remain with the horses, ready to come in with them at the run if needed; the rest of the outfit would approach on foot to within a hundred yards of the wagons, get down in a widely dispersed line opposite them and fire through the wheels at the cattle beyond. After pouring in about twenty rounds each, they must stop firing and work their way round to another position where they could open up again. If the defenders sallied out, Awker opined that they could dodge them easily in the dark. 'We'll pull out then. We'll have done the damage, anyway. You fellars with them hosses had better keep your eyes skinned for them fellars comin' out, d'you hear?'

They heard. Awker also heard a mutter from one of them about wanting a smoke, and he turned on him in fury and told him not to be a damn fool. A cigarette would betray them, right now.

Awker nearly always worked himself into a fury when he felt in the slightest way crossed in his plans.

Iron Jack stole softly behind the dismounted party as they walked stealthily up towards the wagon circle. Already there was an idea simmering in his brain; an idea he'd seen put across a United States army unit down Fort Laramie way by Comanche Indians. And that talk about smoking had triggered off first thoughts of the plan.

After a while Awker gave a soft word of command and his men began to string out in the darkness and get down among the sagebrush. It was obvious by now where the camp was, because of the constant lowing of the cattle penned reluctantly within the wagon circle, and when Iron Jack crouched down he thought he could even see the dim outlines of the vehicles because the thin moon was climbing up behind them.

He held up his hand to test the wind and found it satisfactory. It was blowing down the direction that the line of men had taken. He could hear the last of the men getting into place now and he knew he had to work fast. He stumbled cautiously around until he found a depression that would hide him from sight, then he got down on his knees beside a big clump of dry sage and pulled out his matches.

Carefully cupping the flame, he touched off the tindery brushwood. The second he saw it had taken he leapt out of the hollow and ran like fury up-wind.

He had taken half a dozen yards when he heard a quick gasp of alarm from one of Awker's men. He looked back as he ran. The steady-blowing wind had fanned the flame into a sudden fire, lighting up the prairie astonishingly. Even as he looked he saw the flames leap from bush to bush, spreading rapidly and climbing higher and filling the night with a roaring sound as it burnt up the desert-dry sage.

Awker's voice roared out in fury, 'Who did that, goddammit?'

Then a barrage of fire started from across under the wagons. Iron Jack saw red flame spurt in a line that was two hundred yards long. He went crashing on to his face just as the first spinning lead bullets screamed over his head.

# CHAPTER THREE

Iron Jack got a mouthful of dust in his hurry to get low under cover, but immediately he was down he began to take risks on a shot hitting him. He lifted his head and looked back.

The fire was blowing hard now, lighting up the night sky vividly. Trapped between it and the wagons, Awker and his men must have been plainly silhouetted against the crimson leaping light, and the grim teamsters under their vehicles let them have it.

Several raiders fell, crying with pain, before Awker's men got over their panic and leapt for any cover that the undulating desert offered them. Iron Jack saw some of them jump through the fire where it was burning thin, to get into the protective darkness beyond. Awker was one of them, and Iron Jack heard his furious, bellowing voice shouting to his men to follow him. The raiders had been routed without a shot being fired by them, and their chief didn't like it.

The barrage of firing if anything intensified as the wagoners saw their quarry escaping through the flames. Some more of Awker's men stopped lead, and either got through the fire limping or fell in their tracks. Awker didn't stop to help the fallen. He was shouting for the horses to be brought up; he was only concerned with his own skin at that moment . . . .

Iron Jack suddenly realized that his own skin was in danger. The firing had ceased from across at the wagons, and he could hear the loud, exultant voices of the defenders, celebrating over their victory. Then he heard hoofs racing towards him and realized that he was directly in line with the advancing horses that were being brought up for Awker and his men.

He began to crawl away, but probably crawled into a worse position because all around him in the darkness now men were blundering – Awker's men, crashing through the sagebrush in a hurry to get to the trail and their horses.

Iron Jack was caught between running horses on one side and running men on the other.

He began to run towards the horses, shouting hoarsely as he did so. Not for nothing did he play poker, and just now he put up the biggest bluff of his life.

It came off. All around him now were the lurching shapes of running men. They were cursing, and when they heard Iron Jack's angry voice they couldn't think it was anyone except one of themselves.

Jud Awker's rough, raging voice bellowed, 'Ride fast, men. We don't want ter git caught in a trap!' Now it was that the darkness held terrors for the attackers – imaginary ones, as it turned out.

Iron Jack heard a horse plunge rapidly away

westward along the dimly discernible trail, and guessed it to be Awker making sure of his own skin. All around him men were catching horses, not concerned whose they were, and clambering up into saddles and urging them away. They were a badly beaten crowd, too beaten even to think of revenge just then.

Iron Jack found himself up against a horse, and promptly swung into the saddle, too. A couple more riderless horses were up against the one he strode, so he reached down and caught them by the curb reins and held on to them when the last of the men mounted and belted up the trail after his companions. A few minutes later Iron Jack found another horse running loose, and it came up to them and he caught it and that gave him four horses that he had never owned before.

He rode down towards the firelight, shouting all the way, and when he saw that he had been recognized he spurred across the flame-lit prairie up to the wagons. His arrival was greeted with a buzz of delighted talk, especially when they saw him with the four horses. But Iron Jack had things to do and he started to shout orders.

'Get out an' put that fire out,' he ordered. If the wind changed it might blow the prairie fire on to the precious wagon circle, and he wanted draught oxen, not roast beef. He also called out, 'An' while you're doin' it, keep your eyes skinned fer dead an' wounded of that gang. There's some about.'

The men ran for sacks which they wetted and then raced across to the spreading fire. Wagonmaster Thompson came riding up on a horse, demanding, 'You sure it's safe, Jack?'

'Safe? Hell, them Awker's men won't come back tonight – not the way they was headin',' Iron Jack assured him. He told the trail boss what had happened.

'I changed my mind about pickin' up a prisoner an' bringin' him in, Tommy. I heard Awker's voice, an' that was good enough for me. Now we know the enemy, and – hully gee, when we get to Virginie City, are we goin' ter make 'em pay fer them dead oxen!'

Two days later the big Kansas freight haulage outfit came rolling into Crooked Ford, on the outskirts of the thriving, bustling, developing mining town of Virginia City. They brought with them four wounded prisoners, sullen men who didn't open their mouths when questions were asked about their employers . . . the dead had been buried back on the prairie.

Iron Jack rode in with the prisoners with a strong escort of a dozen out-riders. Virginia City had a sheriff, though no one took much notice of him then, and a citizens' vigilance committee was in process of being set up to bring in the law that was notable for its absence in the town. Iron Jack knew that the sheriff hadn't much power, but all the same he handed over the prisoners for trial and was blunt to the shyster behind the silver star in order to make sure that they did come up before a judge.

'Brother, you're responsible,' he told the sheriff. 'If them fellars manage ter heist outa your jail, you'll have the Kansas outfit gunnin' fer you, get me?'

The sheriff shot off his mouth to show he wasn't to be pushed around. 'You Kansas people think you're gonna run the West now, don't you?'

'We're gonna see justice is done, when things affect us,' Iron Jack said rudely. He'd never liked this two-timing sheriff, and he was at pains now to show his distaste of the office-holder.

The sheriff did a lot of talking, but he was impressed and locked the men up in the two steel-fronted cells that his jail boasted. In this unruly town he kept his job by yielding to the stronger elements in the place. At this moment the big, ex-Texas Ranger was one of those same strong elements.

Then Iron Jack went to look for Awker. He wanted a show-down, and he thought he'd get it over with before the stage arrived with Ann Caudry. Ann wouldn't like to see him in any trouble.

The lamps were being lit, all along the main street of Virginia City, though it wasn't dark yet. Lamp oil was a fabulous price, but the saloons and gambling hells that lit them up so early were making fortunes every night from the strike-crazy miners and they could afford to pay for it.

They were looking in at their third saloon when a growing roar down the street brought them hurriedly on to the board sidewalk again. All at once the street was crowded with rough, bearded miners, watching down in the distance where the trail came in front Crooked Ford.

A lone rider was riding in, hell for leather, racing his mount down the street until it came to the rest station of the Pony Express Company. A fresh horse was being held, saddled and bridled and ready for the trail to Carson City. They saw the mailrider, a spare, lightweight of a man, tired after a relay of seventy-five miles that had involved a change of six different horses, yet find strength enough to leap down and pull from his saddle the *mochila* to which was fastened the *cantinas* – four leather pouches which contained the five-dollars-a-time letters for the Pacific Coast.

Iron Jack was as delighted as the miners, cheering in the street. 'That's the fastest ride yet, Shep,' he told the wagonmaster's assistant. 'The mail's a day ahead of time. At this rate he'll do it in just over eight days to Sacramento.'

Even to Iron Jack, who had always believed in the Pony Express, it was staggering that the near-two thousand miles journey could be accomplished in little more than a week's time.

He began to push his way through the crowd of miners, many of them settling the usual bet on the time of arrival of the mail in Virginia City. Shep called, 'Where you goin', Jack?'

'To see what mail there is for me,' Iron Jack called back. He had forgotten Shep Clayton and the outriders for the moment. 'Hang around. I'll find you.'

He had an idea that with that mail would be a letter for himself from Ann, and he badly wanted to hear from her. She must be getting pretty close to Virginia City now, and her letter would tell him how near she was.

As he ran up with a crowd of men towards the rest station, he was in time to see the Virginia mails go into the *cantinas* – saw the *mochila*, that square of leather, go sailing over the saddle and then a fresh rider go leaping into his seat and hurtle away towards the mountain track. A cheer went up, for the arrival of the west-bound Pony Express rider was a big moment in the lives of these hardworking mining folk.

Iron Jack slapped the weary, trail-dusty rider on the back and called, 'Nice goin', Danny. Some day the Continent's gonna be crossed in less than a week, the way you fellars are goin' on.'

Danny grinned. Riding the mails was a tough job, and few men could stand the pace; but there wasn't a man that would lightly throw in as an Express rider, because there was a thrill attached to every day's mad dash across country, leaping from horse to horse at the way stations, that no other job could provide.

Iron Jack followed the mail inside the office. A clerk looked up, recognized him, and went on sorting the letters. The big boss had almost given up hope, when two letters were pitched across the desk towards him. 'Two fer you, boss,' the clerk said, glad to please the Pacific Coast manager of both the Pony Express Company and this new venture that was coming in, the freight haulage business of Russell, Majors and Waddell.

Iron Jack saw feminine handwriting under the oiled silk wrapping of the letter and opened that one first. It was from Ann.

'Dear Jack,' she wrote, 'I'm told there will be a Pony Express rider coming in to Austin within a day or so, and I am going to leave this letter, hoping the Express will get it to you before I arrive in Virginia City.

'We lost some time covering the salt flats outside

Salt Lake City, because a late storm came and churned up the trail for us. Nevertheless I am assured that we shall be in Virginia City on Thursday afternoon, and I am looking forward to seeing you. Hurriedly, Yours, Ann.'

Thursday! That was tomorrow afternoon! His pulse raced at the prospect of seeing the girl again. He put the letter carefully into the breast pocket of his shirt, then less carefully ripped open the second letter.

It was from the company's headquarters at Atchison, Kansas. There were some instructions for him, and then a friendly paragraph about the new haulage business.

'Everything depends on you, Jack,' Will Russell, senior partner in the firm, wrote to him. 'That Pony Express Company is more expensive than we thought it would be, and we'll be ruined if we have to rely upon mail receipts. So, if we are to keep the idea alive, we'll have to build up a big Pacific Coast haulage business. The Pony Express is a fine advertisement for us, of course, and must secure us a lot of valuable goodwill. Nevertheless we must ask you to put your back into the haulage business; keep the expenses down, and show us a profit so that we can continue the Pony Express Company.'

He put that letter into his pocket, too. He began to walk back through the darkening street, and he was thinking what the partners would say when he wrote them that they had lost several hundred valuable head of oxen in the recent night stampede. It was a bitter blow – apart from the value of the beasts, there was the loss to the company of their practical resources. Wagons weren't any good without beasts to pull them.

The crowds had drifted from the street by now, leaving only a few loiterers on the lamp-lit sidewalk. The saloons were noisy again, and Iron Jack heard the tinkle of a piano and the rather strident voice of some female entertainer lifted in song. Hoarse applause followed it.

He sought for the saloon, outside of which he had left his companions, but he hadn't taken much note of the place and now was unsure in searching for it. He decided upon one, loud with raucous voices, and passed into the smoke-filled atmosphere.

Immediately he came in some men rose and went out hurriedly. Iron Jack didn't see them; he was looking for familiar faces. But Shep Clayton and his men weren't there, and when he was assured on that point, the Pacific Coast boss turned to leave the saloon.

Outside on the board sidewalk he halted to let his eyes get used to the darkness. He heard a swift rush of feet towards him, and instinctively he crouched, not knowing what it was but suspecting danger to himself.

Even so, the first vicious fist caught him on the side of his head and sent him reeling. He felt himself falling into the dust of the street, and his head was dazed from the effects of that blow. Then they were on to him.

Three or four big, burly men drove into him with fists and feet. He rolled before the storm, protecting his head with his arms, and somehow got upright again. He tried to get his gun, but they were all over him, holding him while others hit him. He realized that that was the object of these men – they were beating him up, not intending to kill him. They were giving him the thrashing of his life.

Somehow he staggered clear for a second, and his fists stabbed out, hitting and hurting. There was blood running from a cut over his right eye, and his mouth felt bruised and puffed and smarting. His strength was leaving him, but he fought back savagely, his breath heaving labouredly from the exertion of the moment.

They came tearing back at him, snarling, and cursing with unabated persistence, trying to get him down on to the ground again so that they could get their boots into him. Iron Jack, desperately trying to beat them back, felt a hand claw down the front of his shirt. It gripped on his breast pocket and held, and he found himself being dragged down. With all his remaining strength he threw himself backwards, trying to get out of that grip. He heard the pocket tear and come away in his assailant's hand, and he reeled back free. Their fists were at him again in a moment, but the force of his backwards movement got him against a wall ... somehow his hand was able to get down now to the Colt in his belt.

One of the thugs must have caught the flash of light upon steel and cried out a warning. 'Look out, he's got his gun!'

Iron Jack, bleeding against that wall, felt rather than saw his opponents pull quickly away from him into the darkness. They turned and started to run, and within a few yards were lost to sight.

At that, cautious spectators began to crowd

forward from the doorways. In Virginia City it wasn't healthy to horn in on anyone else's quarrel, and people said you lived long if you followed the principle of minding your own business.

Iron Jack wiped his face with his shirt sleeve, still standing with his back to the wall and recovering his breath. When he had recovered his wind sufficiently he went walking forward into the light from the saloon window, and at once Shep Clayton came pushing his way through the crowd.

'What'n heck, Jack?' he exclaimed. 'You bin pickin' a fight?'

'What do you think, Shep?' Iron Jack somehow infused a little note of humour into his voice. 'Think I get like this through eatin' hominy grits?'

Shep ignored the badinage and pulled the big boss into the saloon. Men crowded round to have a look at Iron Jack, who was certainly a sight. He saw himself in a mirror, and winced at his own appearance. Then he remembered that Ann Caudry was coming in by stage next day, and he felt depressed that she should see him with such a cut-up face.

Shep's men came up one by one and gathered round their boss. They were itching for trouble, red-raw with anger at the thought that their comrade should receive such a beating up.

One growled, 'Who did it, Jack? We'll go an' tear off their heads, so help me!'

Iron Jack mopped his face to staunch the cuts. He made a guess. 'I'd say I ran into some boys who got scared by that fire last night. Mebbe it's got around that I started it, so when they saw me alone in the dark they pitched in to give me a beatin' up. Just mean revenge, I reckon.'

Shep said, 'Then you won't go walkin' around alone in the dark agen, Jack.'

Iron Jack rose. His face was hard under his bruises. 'Let's go,' he said. 'We'll finish what we set off to do. C'mon, let's see of we c'n find that loud-mouthed, dirty-tempered li'l Jud Awker.'

He started to lead the way out of the saloon, the others following. They were ripe for trouble, and the watching spectators thought they'd go along to witness it. Apart from the arrival of the Pony Express, Virginia City could be a very dull town.

Then Shep Clayton, right by the door, said, 'Looks like you lost part of your shirt, Jack.'

Iron Jack looked down, then came to an abrupt halt. His shirt pocket had been torn completely away. His hand rose in an ineffectual gesture, as if to grip the pocket with its letters. Then Jack Irons went striding out into the street to look for the missing letters.

He didn't find them.

At that moment a big, flashy, gambler-type man, with an unceasing smile on his good-looking face, was reading them, and they appeared to give him a great deal of satisfaction.

# CHAPTER FOUR

They found Jud Awker in town, drinking with some of his men down at the Silver Dollar saloon. Awker had been warned that big Iron Jack was looking for him, but he was in no mood to run away. Awker liked trouble, and he thought that he could hold his own with the prize bullies standing around him. Jud Awker only picked men who were big and rough and without conscience.

The other drinkers in the Silver Dollar got the whisper that there was likely to be gun-play, and they began to find all manner of reasons for leaving the saloon in a hurry, so that when Iron Jack came in through the batwings he found the Awker men in sole possession of the bar.

The Pacific Coast boss halted just inside the saloon, his men crowding in behind him. The interested spectators who had followed all down the street, now numbering a couple of hundred at least, ran for strategic watching places at the windows. To them this looked like the beginnings of one first-class dog-fight!

The Silver Dollar proprietor saw the stiffened

attitudes of the Awker men at the bar, saw the threatening crouch of the newcomers, and began to take down his precious mirrors and glasses from the shelves behind him. He shouted that he didn't want trouble in the Silver Dollar, and if there was any he'd have the sheriff in on them. That made the spectators at the windows laugh. Their sheriff would be tucked up in bed now, if they knew him.

Little Jud Awker, broad, sturdy and tough, was drinking as Iron Jack walked slowly across to him. Awker's bullies edged away, so that their gun hands were free for sudden movement.

Iron Jack stood in front of the rival freight hauler and said, pleasantly, 'You kinda got a roastin' last night, didn't you, Awker?'

It touched the quarrelsome little man on the raw, to be reminded of his previous night's discomfiture. The glass stayed at his lips, but he had stopped drinking now, and his eyes spat hatred at the big man who had turned the tables on him.

Iron Jack continued, just as softly, 'You don't need to tell me it wasn't you, Awker, because I know it was.' By this time Shep Clayton and the out-riders had eased up into a line on either side of him. At the windows the spectators watched, tensed and expectant. The two parties were about even, and that spelt a good fight – if it came off.

'Wal, Awker, you've shown your hand, but I aim ter tell you that you won't keep us out of this territory now. You started it – we'll finish it! You try'n bust us, an' we'll bust you, *sabe?*'

For answer Awker lowered his half-filled whiskey glass. For a second he deliberately twiddled it in his fingers, looking at the swilling yellow liquid. Then he hurled the contents, suddenly and unexpectedly, into the big boss's face.

It was the kind of trick men expected of Jud Awker. Always this happened; always when other men would have proceeded with caution, that vicious, dirty little temper would come boiling over and he did impulsive, distasteful things.

That alcohol got into big Jack Irons' eyes and burnt them; it ran into the wounds on his face and made them seem on fire.

But the big fellow just wiped away the liquid, then suddenly sent his strong brown hands stabbing out to grab Awker by the ears. There was a yell of delight from outside. Awker had to go with his ears. Irons swung him round, then gripped his head, and with the force of that unbalanced movement Jud Awker found himself being lifted right off his feet and hurled on to the bartender, back of the bar. There was a crash as the shelves of glasses came tumbling down on them.

The bartender began to shout again, but his voice was lost in the roar of angry voices as the two freight haulage outfits came clashing together. A few guns came out and popped off but did little damage before they were silenced in a hand-to-hand fight.

The clapboard building shook as fighting men crashed to the ground, or were hurled against the wooden saloon walls. It was the doggondest fight Virginia City had seen since the first days when the town had been thrown open to claimstakers.

Big Jack Irons, in a fury because he had taken

enough punishment from the San Francisco hauler, went across that bar in a dive after his opponent. He sprawled on top of the bartender, then saw Jud Awker pulling away, clambering erect down the length of the bar and drawing his Colt as he did so.

And Awker was murderous, off his head with fury at that moment. Men didn't lay hands on him and live, he was snarling to himself right then. He saw big Jack Irons, tough and fighting mad, following his recent thrashing by Awker's men, and he lifted his gun to blast lead into the Pony Express West Coast chief.

Irons saw the gun – simultaneously saw the irate bartender lift a bottle to smack on to Irons' skull. Big Jack grabbed and all in one movement wrestled the bottle from the bartender's grasp and hurled it at Awker.

The bottle was heavy, because it was a full one, and it crashed into Awker's stomach before his finger tightened on the trigger, and he went reeling back in the agony that comes when a man is forcibly deprived of his wind.

Irons came lurching to his feet. He heard tables crashing over on to the floor, heard chairs splinter as men crashed them on to other men, heard the bellowing din of men savaging each other, shouting with vicious delight one moment – the next yelping with pain as the tables were turned on them.

The big boss got across to Awker before the shorter man could recover and bring his revolver up again. He grabbed Awker's wrist. Awker was short, but he had strength and he battled against that grip and for a few seconds held the bigger man. Then

Irons got impatient and twisted suddenly and smacked Awker's fist on to the edge of the bar and that loosened the grip on the revolver.

Awker roared with pain and went beserk again. Iron Jack fought with him in the narrow confines behind the bar. Then he hurled his opponent out through the gate beyond and they became mixed up in the fighting on the saloon floor. Awker got lost for a moment, but Iron Jack wasn't going to let him out of his sight easily, and dived into the swirling mass of arms and legs and bodies and dragged him out. Then he drove him with his fists to the batwing doors – and kicked him out into the street.

Iron Jack knew his opponent and knew that that sort of treatment would hurt Jud Awker more than anything. He had publicly whipped the West Coast haulier and humbled him in front of his men and these citizens of Virginia City. Like many other little men, Jud Awker couldn't forgive a beating, but more especially couldn't overlook the blow to his pride that an open defeat brought behind it.

Iron Jack stood panting in the lighted doorway, looking down at Awker as he lay sprawling in the yellow lamplight on the dusty roadway. Awker was hardly moving; he had taken a lot of punishment in the last few minutes.

Iron Jack wasn't in much better condition, because this fight had come too soon upon the thrashing he had just received, and his struggle with Awker had re-opened his wounds and set his bruises to hurting worse than ever.

He went back into the saloon, however, determined to finish the job. Several men were flat out on the floor now, and others were reeling as if they weren't much more conscious. Irons grabbed one of the men, turned him and saw he was an Awker man, and slammed him head first through the batwings out after his boss.

It seemed good tactics, so he did it to another reeling *hombre*. Then his out-riders got on to the idea and began pitching Awker's bullies out on top of their boss. At that moment the Kansas men were in an invincible mood, so filled with fury were they by the treachery of two night attacks upon them. It would have needed more than an equal number of bullies to defeat them that night.

When the last Awker man had been thrashed and tossed out on to the pile, Irons and his men stood out on the sidewalk to recover. The bartender got the door-bar down and locked them all out while they were standing there, so they couldn't go back in for a drink as some of the thirsty, jubilant out-riders were already proposing.

One by one the Awker crowd got to their feet and staggered sullenly away. Awker himself had suffered from the weight on top of him and had to be carried off.

A man came edging up to big Jack Irons as he leaned against a roof support, recovering. He was just an ordinary sort of man, big and rough and middle-aged.

He said, 'Brother, he'll kill you for that.'

'Awker?'

'Awker. Him an' his outfit try ter run this town, an' there's plenty here that'll get a kick outa seein' him pitched on to his bad-tempered li'l head.

57

Awker'll know that, an' he won't forgive you, mister.'

Iron Jack said, shortly, 'I don't want his forgiveness. He's got worse comin' to him ef he tries any more tricks agen this outfit. He only got what he asked for.'

'Sure, sure.' The man spoke quickly, and Iron Jack had a feeling he was a friend. He dropped his voice. 'Look, Mister Pony Express Man, there's some folks that are sick of the way a few men like Awker run Virginia City. We'll be glad when you start haulin' ter San Francisco, 'cause we're tired of bein' bled by the Awker line. But we'd be even more glad ef a few handy-fisted men like you an' your crowd joined us.'

'Us?' Iron Jack stared at the man.

The man paused, watching Iron Jack's face in the yellow lamplight; when he did speak it was guardedly. 'Yeah, us. A few fellars like myself that's sick an' tired of mob law an' disorder. We figger it's time we got ourselves a sheriff – a good one. Someone who won't stand by an' see good citizens shoved around an' knocked over the head an' robbed.'

'You got anythin' ter do with this vigilance movement I keep hearin' talk about, friend?' Iron Jack interrupted.

'Mebbe.'

Iron Jack sighed. 'You'd get my support, only I figger I've got my hands full enough fighting the Awker bunch without takin' on as a vigilante, too.'

'That's kinda disappointin',' the man said, but he didn't pursue the subject. Perhaps he recognized the finality of the decision in Iron Jack's tone. He did say, though – ' Mebbe you'll be glad of the vigilantes, someday.'

Iron Jack said, 'Mebbe.'

Then the man showed he was a friend. His voice dropped to a whisper. 'Look, Jack, let me tell you somethin' I've heard. They're sayin', round the town, that Awker's out to bust the Express. There's talk that he's takin' on men specially fer that purpose, an' the next rider ain't gonna get past Virginia City.'

Iron Jack's eyes grew hard. 'That all you know?'

'That's all. An' I'm tellin' you 'cause I'm kinda friendly towards the Pony Mail.'

Irons said, 'Thanks, brother. I won't forget the tip.'

He swung round, in a hurry now. He jerked his head and Shep Clayton came up quickly. Shep was looking pleased with himself.

Iron Jack spoke softly in his ear. 'Shep, I've a job fer you. There's a rumour around town that Jud Awker's out to stop the mail goin' through. I guess he figgers ef we lose any mail we'll not be allowed to carry fer the Government, an' that's goin' ter cost the company a packet of money.'

Too much, he knew; even now the company was losing heavily on the experiment, and without Government mail there would be no chance of ever breaking even.

'What do you want me ter do, Jack?'

'You hang around town, Shep, with three or four of the boys. Keep your ears skinned an' see ef you c'n find out any of the plans. I'm ridin' out to talk with Thompson about this matter.'

Leaving Shep and his picked men to go off into the crowd, Iron Jack rode quickly back through the darkness with the rest of the weary, battered but triumphant out-riders to the camp.

The wagonmaster, glasses on his nose, reading with the aid of a hurricane lamp under his wagon, exclaimed when he saw the big boss. 'The heck, Jack, you bin knocked down by a cow?'

'I got other names fer 'em,' Iron Jack said grimly. He sat down and told Thompson about the night's happenings. When he'd concluded he said, 'You've got a lot of spare men on your hands now, Tommy. You've got over a third of your wagons without beasts, so you won't want drivers for 'em. We c'n get hosses from the Carson City depot for 'em, an' we'll use 'em to bust up any plans of the Awker mob. We'll fix about a dozen teamsters at every rest an' way station within fifty miles of Virginia City, either way. They'll be on hand, then, wherever trouble breaks out.'

Thompson said, 'Doesn't the next east-bound mail go through about noon tomorrow?'

Iron Jack snapped his fingers in annoyance. He knew what Thompson had in mind. They couldn't get the horses through from Carson City in that time. He sat and considered, and then made up his mind.

'Send half a dozen of your men right away to Carson City to bring in all the spare hosses we've got out there.' They had to have horses, and he knew it would be hopeless trying to get any here in Virginia City – saddle horses were almost beyond price in this community, and those who owned wouldn't sell. So it had to be Carson City, and a hope that the stables there, which served all the western sector of the Pony Express service, would have plenty of mounts in condition to be used.

'Mebbe you'll have time; mebbe they won't go fer the next rider but for the west-bound one that comes through on Sat'day.' Thompson was trying to be consoling.

Iron Jack said, 'Mebbe,' but he couldn't take any chances. He said, 'Get your spare teamsters to walk out to the way stations, some east an' some west of the town. They won't like it, but they'll go ef they think there's a fight at the end of the trail for 'em. They're no good in town, I figger, so get 'em out. We'll run the hosses out to 'em an' move 'em to other further stations along the trail just as soon as your boys come in from Carson City.'

It was the best they could do at such short notice, and Thompson went striding round the camp, giving orders. Half a dozen out-riders, grumbling because another night's sleep had to be forfeited, saddled up and took the night trail west. The teamsters selected for the long walk the next day did a lot of hearty cussing, so much so that it kept the tired and bruised boss of theirs awake for quite two minutes after he'd got down in his blanket. Teamsters hated to walk, especially in these dry, desert regions around Virginia City.

Shep Clayton and his men rode back into camp just before dawn. They were very weary and they had news – some was valuable, some merely irritating.

Big Iron Jack was wakened and climbed stiffly out into the chill of the dark morning. He felt bad, sore all over from the drubbing he'd had. Nevertheless he crossed over to a fire without complaint, and stood and warmed himself while

Shep gave the news.

'The Awker crowd didn't let their pals stay long in jail,' he said grimly. 'They stick together, them fellars; that's what makes 'em so dangerous.'

'What happened?'

'Around midnight half a dozen *hombres* hitched ropes to the bars of them cells and pulled the side of the buildin' clean out with their hosses. Then they walked in, collected their wounded, an' rode off without out a shot bein' fired after 'em.' His voice was bitter. 'Ef I'd have bin at that end of the town I'd have blasted off at 'em!' he swore.

'What were you doin'?'

'Me'n some of the boys got an idea after you left.' He shot a quick glance at his boss. 'Mebbe you wouldn't have approved of it.' He rolled himself a quirly with tired fingers. It had been a distasteful job and he wanted to forget about it. 'Late at night we saw a fellar that was p'inted out as an Awker man in on the spree. We watched him get so drunk he didn't know where he was goin', an' then we led him out to a piece of waste land by Terrigo Flats an' asked him a few questions.'

'I see.' Iron Jack understood.

'We asked what Jud Awker's plans were, but he was stubborn an' wouldn't talk fer a long time. We had to get rough afore he'd tell us.'

Iron Jack shook his head. ' Shep,' he said, 'I don't like that sort of work. You don't do it agen, *sabe*?' He didn't like to think of a drunk being knocked around to make him talk. That was hoodlum stuff, the kind of trick he'd expect from Jud Awker. Shep was young, and it was the kind of thing a hot-headed, loyal young chap might do.

Shep looked sullen. He growled, 'OK, Jack, but it worked. The fellar used his tongue a lot.'

'Let's hear it, then.' Might as well use the information, now it had been obtained.

Shep squatted on his haunches and lit up from the red embers of the fire. He spoke deliberately. 'Awker's made a vow that nothin's goin' west to San Francisco of the Russell, Majors and Waddell concern – neither mail nor freight wagons. An' no mail's goin' ter be allowed into Virginie City from the Pacific, either. The drunk said Awker had a gamblin' man who'd bin recruitin' from the diggin's over in Sacramento – he'd bin doing it right from the day the Pony Express had started to run. He said Awker's got nigh on a hundred men camped in the Tahoe Hills, ready ter move on to the trail an' block it to our outfit.'

'The Tahoe Hills.' Once before there'd been a clumsy attempt to hold up the mails in that wild and desolate region. It was just the place for a hold-up; the terrain was so rough that an army could camp within a few hundred yards of the trail without anyone being the wiser.

Shep said, deliberately, 'They're movin' in today, ter stop the east-bound mail carrier. That's what the drunk said, anyway.'

Iron Jack thought of the men at his disposal – of his mounted men, because the foot-slogging teamsters would never get out to the Tahoe Hills in time to be useful. All told he would have less than a dozen available, now that six out-riders had already pulled out for distant Carson City. That wasn't many, not against Awker's army of nearly a hundred ruffians.

He sent Shep and his men to get a couple of hours sleep, then went and wakened the camp cooks and ordered early breakfast for the men who would be pulling out at dawn.

With first light he was away, having left instructions with Shep to follow with the out-riders. His big black stallion tore up the miles as if it could go on all day. It was one of the finest horses in America, and had been given to Iron Jack by his employers for coming to them in the first place with the Pony Express project. These days he sure was glad of that stallion.

Three hours later he was in the rough country of the Tahoe Hills. There was a way station here, with a couple of men to look after the four horses that were used in change-overs. The station had been attacked once, by Jud Awker and his men, with the result that the new men in charge were the toughest Irons could find, and they never moved a yard without picking up a rifle and pushing off the safety catch.

He rode down into the valley where the station – a stout log cabin – was situated. He rode cautiously, not wanting a bullet from his own men, and also careful because of the possibilities of ambush.

One of the hostlers came to the door, recognizing him and waving. He was a big, flat-faced, ex-prize-fighter from 'Frisco.

Irons rode up and dismounted. The other hostler came out then and attended to his horse. Irons asked, 'Seen any suspicious moves around here lately, Babe?'

Babe knew what he was talking about and screwed up his leathery face significantly as he growled, 'Nope – or I'd have done somethin' about it.'

'Against a hundred men – all toughies from the diggin's?'

That brought Babe's eyes wider than they'd been since he was a boy. 'A hundred? That's a tidy lot.'

Iron Jack said, 'You couldn't miss that number, ef they came along the trail.'

'They haven't bin along this trail, not so many men.' This wasn't the main highway into the Sierras, but a short, though hard going, cut across a great bend in the main trail. Only a few prospectors on foot used it, most other traffic following the easier trail to the north of them. An influx of a hundred men into the territory would have been noticeable, as Iron Jack had commented.

Then Babe looked at Iron Jack's bruised features and said, 'Looks like you already had a fight with a hundred toughies, Jack? Or was it a mule tried to kick your head off?'

Iron Jack said they weren't mules, the ones that had marked his face for him, though they sure could kick like four-legged animals. He wasn't in the mood for humour. He was worried about the mail; by now it must be within an hour's run of them – possibly less – and if there was an ambush he might already have ridden unsuspectingly through it or again it might be set miles westwards from here. These Tahoe Hills provided perfect cover for his enemies.

He was also worrying about the stage arriving with Ann that afternoon. He wanted to be back to meet her, because he didn't like to think of her being on her own even for a short while in that rough mining town. Some of the miners, especially those in drink, were uncouth and unpleasant to unaccompanied girls.

He thought, 'The Babe doesn't help at all. Now what do I do?'

He decided to leave his stallion, to be picked up on his way back, and he ordered the Babe to saddle up a spare mount. It was a beautiful mount, one of the express ponies, resting between trips. He mounted and swung off westwards.

The Babe called, 'S'long, boss. Keep your eye open fer Injuns.'

Iron Jack had trotted a good hundred yards from the little log way-station before that remark became significant to him. Then he turned and galloped his horse back to the surprised Babe and his companion hostler. He leaned from the saddle and demanded, 'What did you mean by that remark, Babe?'

'About Injuns?' The Babe's mind caught up slowly with the question.

'Yeah. What Injuns?'

The Babe blinked. 'Jes' that Hank an' I figger thar's Injuns movin' across the trail. We saw plenty smoke this mornin', way up the side of Tahoe Peak. That's the way Injuns always strike north, we've bin told.'

Iron Jack's bruised face surveyed him pityingly for a moment, then he said, 'Why didn't you tell me that before, Babe?' He laughed shortly. 'There's no Injuns moving up the mountains at this time o' year, fellar – they go up at the end of March to get away from the heat of the plains, an' they come down in

Fall when it's beginnin' ter get too cold for 'em. But you won't find big parties on the move in between times.'

Babe gawked. 'Then you don't think they're Injuns?'

Iron Jack said, 'I think I'll go an' have a look at 'em, anyway.' He was looking for a large body of men encamped along this trail, and this sounded like the quarry he was after. He got the Babe to show him whereabouts they had seen smoke that morning, and then he went away at a gallop.

He rode fast now, knowing that time was running against him. All the same he rode with caution, pausing on every eminence of the trail to survey the land ahead. Once, looking high into the mountains ahead, he thought he saw a tiny dust cloud, as from some fast-riding horseman. He thought, 'That'll be the east-bound mail,' and it made him want to get on much faster.

At last he came to that part of the trail which skirted the steep wooded slopes of the Tahoe Peak. It must have been near here that those 'Indians' had had their fires that morning.

Suddenly he spotted the ambush. It was cleverly laid, and he thought that if the Babe hadn't given him an idea where to look for it, he'd never have spotted it.

The trail here ran for miles along a shelf that protruded from the steep mountainside; below was a very steep drop into a winding, wooded valley along which ran a mountain stream.

Iron Jack spotted horses tucked into a fold in the hillside, saw men lying behind rocks and bushes along the edge of the track.

The only trouble was – *the men saw him at the same time*!

# CHAPTER FIVE

Iron Jack knew that the rifles were covering him as he rode on to that ambush. But there was no turning back now, for if he tried to turn on that narrow trail the action would for certain look suspicious and bring lead hurtling after him. Anyway, he wanted to get through to warn his pony rider.

He drooped in the saddle, bringing his horse down to a slow jog-trot, let his head slide downwards and sideways, so that his broad-brimmed hat hid his features. He was going to try to bluff his way through.

He figured he had a good chance of getting away with it. They wouldn't want to start any trouble at this moment, which might sound a warning to the advancing Pony Express rider, and he reckoned he would probably pass unrecognized if these were the bullies recruited over on the Pacific Coast.

He thought, with a grim smile, anyway that beating up he'd had to his face must pretty well alter his appearance even to people who had seen him before.

But it wasn't a nice feeling, riding steadily down into that trap, knowing that he was Target No. 1 for the Awker crowd, anyway. The stillness seemed to grip him, so that he held his breath as his ears strove to catch some betraying sound. He rode on . . . he was nearly level with them . . . then he was past.

But that was the worst part of it. He rode in agony, gooseflesh on his back, tremors of nausea riding up and down his stomach as he anticipated a cowardly bullet in the back as a result of belated recognition.

Yet none came. His bluff had come off. They weren't interested in west-bound traffic; these men had received orders to stop the east-bound Pony Express rider only.

He was through. Once round a bend along the shelf he kicked his horse into speed and rode flat out to meet the Pony Express rider.

They met about three miles above the ambush. Here the trail that ran along the shelf dipped down to cross the tumbling mountain stream that ran between a straggle of pines and cedars. Iron Jack saw the pony rider carefully walking his horse through the stream, treacherous with its green-covered, slippery round stones. He saw him pause to let the mount have a well-earned drink – a short drink, though the horse would have stayed and guzzled its belly full.

Then the rider was across, crouching once again in his saddle, and sending that mighty roan plummeting up the slope like some Eastern express train.

Iron Jack put his horse across the track, because he knew that the express rider wouldn't halt unless he was forced to stop. He sat with his hand in the air, empty palm facing the man.

The express rider saw him, hesitated, and then pulled hard on the reins. He was unarmed, like all the other express riders, depending for safety upon the speed of his fine horse ... that was why the ambush along this narrow trail was so well laid – the mail rider wouldn't be able to turn aside and take to the open country, because there was only a precipitous drop and a rocky mountainside at the point where the trap was laid.

Iron Jack shouted, 'It's me – Jack Irons. There's a trap laid for you down along the trail.'

The man, a small, hunched fellow who rode like a professional jockey, came nearer, recognized the Pacific Coast boss and relaxed. Iron Jack cantered up to him.

'There's a mob of Awker's men layin' fer you, two – three miles back along the trail.' The rider knew of Awker and his hostility towards the Pony Express and its parent company back in Kansas. Iron Jack continued, 'There's no way of racin' through, fellar. I figger we've got to try another way round.'

The jockey asked, 'How? There ain't another pass fer fifty miles, an' we ain't got any hosses along it at that. Goin' round would make a coupla days' delay on the run.'

'Sure.' Iron Jack had done some thinking, riding up. He looked down at the sparkling stream that wound between the trees. 'I figger mebbe we could get the mails through down that valley. There's a bit of a path from the old days, afore this trail was cut open ter take the Express.'

'Sneak through?' The little man looked doubtful. He knew the trail like the back of his hand. 'They'll

71

see us, an' we'll be like ducks froze in ice for them guns o' theirs.'

'Us?' asked Iron Jack gently. 'Not you, brother. You're gonna be another kind of duck while I get the mail through – a decoy duck.'

That little, sharp-faced head came round. 'You're takin' the mail from me?' Iron Jack nodded. 'Wal, you're the boss. Ef you say so . . .'

They dismounted and made the change-over with the *mochila*. While they did so, Iron Jack outlined his plan. He explained carefully where the trap was laid, and the jockey recognized the place from the description he gave.

'You ride down until you come to that bend, then you stop, in full sight of 'em. Get down an' look at your hoss's feet, as if it's gone lame. That'll keep their attention on you, an' they won't have time fer sight-seein' down the valley. When you think I'm safely through, turn an' ride back to the last way station.'

The jockey warned, 'I'll be out of gunshot range, but you won't be, boss.'

Iron Jack shrugged. That was a risk he had to take. He had to get the mail through, and he couldn't think of any better plan.

They cantered back to the stream together, and then the Pony Express man waved good-bye, turned and went up on to the shelf trail at a steady hand gallop. The big boss found a little-used path that followed the stream, crossing and recrossing it frequently. It wasn't easy going, but his stallion was sure-footed and went scrambling over the rough parts like a big black puma.

The cover was thin, the trees being no more than an intermittent border down the very bottom of the narrow valley, and several times, looking up, Iron Jack saw the Pony Express rider high up on the trail that was cut alongside the mountain face. The jockey was keeping his pace down, but all the same he was gradually getting further ahead.

Then Iron Jack saw him halt right at the edge of the trail. The big ex-Texas Ranger knew that the little man was showing himself so that he, Iron Jack, would know that he had gone as far as he could. He saw the jockey swing down.

Now was the time for caution. He must be riding right under the ambush in the next quarter of a mile.

He proceeded more cautiously now, knowing that in that stillness any sound he made would rise to the ears of the men above him. He kept the horse at a walk, picking out the soft parts in the trail. He had his rifle poised ready in his hands, and all the time he was glancing upwards, ready to shoot if he saw a face peering down at him. Though shooting wouldn't do him much good – down on that narrow, difficult trail he wouldn't stand an earthly.

Step by step his horse took him right under that ambush. He found he was holding his breath, as if feeling that otherwise that might betray him. Right now the little jockey would be making a play at examining a horse that had gone lame, trying to keep all attention on himself. But would he succeed?

It needed only one person to glance down into the valley for his ruse to be discovered.

Step by step, yard after yard, he kept going. And

suddenly he began to breathe easier. He knew now he must have passed the ambush, knew he must be through and walking away from the enemy.

He was just congratulating himself when he heard a flurry of hoofs along the mountain trail above. Then there was hoarse shouting from many men; and the voices were furious like men who have discovered they have been tricked. A scattered volley of shots sent an echo ringing up the confines of the narrowing valley.

At once Iron Jack sent his horse jumping forward into the best pace he could make along that awkward trail. He was trying to work out what those sounds meant. He thought that perhaps the men in ambush had tired of watching the little jockey fiddle around with an apparently lame horse, and some of them had mounted and gone riding off towards him, perhaps thinking he would be easy to pick up.

Then the jockey must have mounted and gone scooting away along the trail, on a horse that most obviously hadn't gone lame. That shout from the men above told him that they realized they had been tricked.

Iron Jack's plan hadn't quite worked out as he'd intended, but it seemed none the worse for that. Probably right now the men were chasing that little resourceful jockey right into California ... the diversion was certainly keeping the attention from himself.

At which exact moment in his thoughts a bullet kicked up water almost under the nose of his mount.

His horse reared and then kicked out, startled by

the screech as the bullet ricochetted off a stone. Iron Jack fought it down and got it going fast along the valley and then looked back.

High above him and far back behind, silhouetted against the blue sky, a man was standing out on the edge of the shelf. He had a gun to his shoulder and was firing again, for Iron Jack saw the white smoke plume out from the gunbarrel, though he didn't hear where that bullet went to.

The man was shouting, and his voice came faintly down to him. Other men came running to the edge of the shelf and looked down upon the lone rider in the valley bottom. Some of them fired, but the distance was great now, and no harm was done by the spent, droning bullets that came his way.

Then all but one of the men disappeared, and Iron Jack guessed they had gone for their horses.

He crouched on his mount, riding recklessly now along that narrow path. When he came to where it crossed the stream again he sent his horse in a leap clean over it. Seconds – even fractions of seconds – counted now.

While he was down on this rough track the pursuers above, who clearly had guessed at the trick that had been played upon them, would gain steadily upon him; then, when the trails converged, they would shoot him down.

Iron Jack's only chance was to keep ahead of the pursuers long enough to reach the main trail about a couple of miles ahead. Once on the trail he felt that his mount would outdistance any pursuit. It was a good horse and was going easily, and his extra weight would mean nothing to it.

One thing, while they were occupied in racing along that trail they couldn't get a shot in at him down below. For the moment he was safe, even if every yard brought him in nearer to the main trail and so into view of their guns.

His horse went down on a rock slide, recovered and went leaping away again. It lost a few yards, though, and yards might count, soon. Then they found themselves in among knee-high rocks that were jagged and dangerous, and he had to walk his horse through the patch – and that lost more yards. And then they ran into very soft ground, where the stream had spread, and he felt the pace slacken as his mount pulled each leg awkwardly out of the deep ooze.

And that meant more yards lost to the racing posse above.

The trees were thinning, and Iron Jack knew that he was coming out on to the trail. Just another half mile and this path and the mountain trail joined.

Desperately he raced now, bent low along the neck his straining horse. Out of his eye corner he was beginning to see the bobbing heads of many riders as they came hurtling down the shelf trail, only a little above him now.

He groaned to himself when he saw how near they were to him. He'd lost the race! At the present pace, he would converge upon the racing horsemen just where the two trails met. That meant that he was committing suicide, going the way he was.

On an impulse he put the head of his horse to the short steep slope that led up to the trail along the shelf. It was difficult going, but the very impetus of that charge sent them both practically up on to the trail before the momentum gave out. Then his horse fought furiously digging in and straining, heaving up towards the brow. Iron Jack rolled out of the saddle, grabbed rein and heaved back on his heels. Together they got out on to the shelf.

He was in time to see the last of the riders go tearing down the trail in a cloud of dust. He had come out on to their heels, and they had no suspicion of the manoeuvre.

As he swung into his saddle he heard horsemen approaching from higher up the trail. Probably these were the horsemen who had gone in pursuit of the Pony Express rider – and failed to catch him. There was no escape that way.

Iron Jack sent his horse thundering after the posse that was trying to cut him off on the trail below. He gained rapidly on the men. He caught up with the last rider, then held his horse just in the rear. Ahead of him about twenty men flogged their mounts into top speed. They had their guns out, ready to open fire the moment they came in sight of the valley track.

Suddenly they were out in the open, off the shelf and in the valley bottom, where the main trail picked up. At once Iron Jack felt the surprise and consternation in the party. They had expected to run right into him – and the valley trail was empty.

Then they must have decided that Iron Jack had pulled back and was retreating up the valley, and they started to wheel on to the path alongside the fast-running stream. Iron Jack rode in their dust, then, but when he was right up with them, he pulled his horse aside and sent it shooting away along the main trail towards the way station.

Someone must have spotted him right away, for he heard a roar of anger go up from the thwarted men. He heard, too, the crackle of gun-fire, but he was rocketing at such speed that he was beyond Colt range and now at a distance that made rifle fire uncertain.

He heard the thunder of their hoofs as they took up the pursuit; they were a very annoyed bunch of thwarted ambushers, and they were intent on getting revenge on this big man who had outwitted them. He nursed his horse into greater speed, and felt the blood surging into its muscles and knew that they would never catch him.

Then his horse dropped down dead, just as he saw a movement along the winding, wooded trail that dipped up and down through the hilly country ahead of him.

As he shot from his saddle his hand gripped the stock of his rifle and dragged it out of the boot. He went hurtling head first on to the dusty trail, but even as he landed his muscles bunched and he came reeling on to his feet immediately and dived back behind the fallen horse. He was acting automatically, from the fighting instincts of a fighting lifetime, for he was dazed from that rude fall. He couldn't understand why his horse had gone down like that – then, as his head cleared, he saw the wound in its side, and realized that some unlucky shot had come in under the ribs and pierced its gallant heart.

It filled him with fury, for he loved horses and this was a mount in a thousand, as were all these prize

Pony Express mounts. He saw a flurry of hoofs as the Awker mob recognized the menace from his rifle and pulled back on their reins. The trail was for a moment a mad tangle of rearing horses, feet kicking, men pulling round and diving for cover.

Iron Jack let go with every round in the breech, smacking lead into these men who had planned to ambush the mail rider. He did some damage, he knew, in spite of that confusion of movement, for someone yelled out with pain, someone went reeling away in his saddle gripping his shoulder – and someone fell and didn't move when he hit the dust.

It stopped the rush, for a moment. Then Irons saw the rest of the ambushers come racing up – the trail looked packed, as if there were dozens along it, careering in to finish him off. Guns were roaring at him now, and he crouched down behind the horse while he rapidly reloaded. Then he fought back and induced caution by the fury of his fire.

His gun was empty again. This time his opponents had been counting. Iron Jack heard a roar from someone in charge, and at once the whole bunch came wheeling their horses round on the trail to charge him. He threw down his gun and drew out his Colts. They wouldn't do him much good; by the time they were in range they'd be too close for him to stop the rush. All the same, he intended to go out fighting.

Three of the leading horsemen came toppling from their saddles. Then a horse was shot down and there was a mighty pile-up in the centre of the trail. Iron Jack looked in astonishment, because this wasn't the result of any of his shooting. He saw the

Awker men rein in in astonishment . . . realized they were staring past him.

He rolled over, grabbing for his rifle and stuffing in a couple of rounds while he did so.

He saw horsemen racing up behind him, firing from the saddle. They were light men, hardy men who seemed part of their horses, unlike these heavier opponents who looked what they were – miners stuck up on horseflesh.

They seemed to be acting on a plan. Suddenly they reined in their mounts – he saw there were about a dozen of them, and one looked like Shep Clayton – and began to pour in a heavy fire at the surprised Awker men.

But one man came through and it was Shep Clayton, he came hurtling like a bullet down the trail towards where Jack Irons lay behind his fallen horse. Right on top of him Shep pulled hard round and his horse nearly fell over with the suddenness of that turn.

Shep bellowed, 'Jump, Jack – jump!' And at that the big boss came up from the ground like a sprinter starting a race. He reached and grabbed the precious *mochila* from off the fallen horse, then dived and caught a stirrup leather. And then his legs bounded in giant strides as he was dragged back by the racing horse towards the rest of his out-riders.

They were within twenty yards of them when the miners recovered from their surprise and opened up a savage hail of fire. Shep Clayton was hit twice, both times in the left arm. Irons lost a lump of flesh out of his thigh that put an end to his running. And the horse crashed down kicking, hit somewhere on its legs, and all three of them lay sprawled in the trail within the fire from those savage gunmen.

# CHAPTER SIX

Someone came crashing from his horse, leaping forward and grabbing the wounded Iron Jack by the scruff of the neck and dragging him frantically in among the horses. The big boss was still tightly clutching the *mochila*. After all he'd gone through, he didn't intend to let that go!

He yelled with pain as rough hands grabbed him by the legs and hurled him up behind a rider, but he knew time was precious – the enemy was in far greater force than his own gallant band of out-riders.

He saw Shep come through on his own and claw his way up behind another rider. The air was filled with the din of guns crashing fire, of men cursing when they were empty, and snarling savage words of defiance as they got them reloaded and firing again. In his nose was the familiar smell of gunpowder. And all about them rose the white smoke from the rifles and the dust where the hoofs of the terrified horses kicked into the dry mountain trail.

They pulled away, the two double-loaded horses, and went at full pelt on towards the way station.

The other out-riders pulled in behind to cover their slower companions with gunfire. Back of them the big Awker outfit came on at a run, furious to see their enemy escape after the thrashing they'd unexpectedly received. It had been a bad day for them – the ambushers had themselves run into an ambush, however unexpectedly it had been laid.

They got even worse medicine in that pursuit. The trail was narrow, and that meant their big force had to bunch. After a while those men out front realized they were shields for their slower companions. The out-riders were pretty good marksmen, used to hunting and firing from the saddle, and they kept wounding and hurting the enemy.

So after a time those sullen miners from over the Sierras began to compete for second and even third place in that race – pulling in a little so as to let someone else get in front. And no one wanted to. So very soon the race was over – the pursuit began to fall steadily backwards, out of range.

When they saw the way station at last, the Awker mob was an uncertain lot of sore and angry horsemen a quarter of a mile to their rear.

A fine, fresh horse was saddled, standing out before the way station, ready to take on the mail. Jack Irons shouted to a lithe young out-rider, 'Hey, Kit, take it – it's yours as far as Virginie City.' In Virginia City was the rest station, where jockeys normally changed over.

Kit Brackenridge, an immigrant fresh out from Cumberland, England, whooped with delight. This sure was a day for him! Now he was riding the mail like a legendary Pony Express man!

He came off his horse at full gallop; his feet took up the pace and he ran; hurling the *mochila* on to the fresh mount and gaining the saddle almost in the same second. They saw him crash away up the hillside, and they could hear his shouts of delight as he felt the mighty animal respond to his urgings. He was a very proud young man, then.

Irons wheeled his horsemen behind the stout cabin. They came leaping down, behind the cover, and went jumping to where they could see down the trail. Their rifles were lifted, ready to burst into fire.

But the Awker outfit had had enough. They knew they couldn't take that solid, well-defended position without heavy losses to themselves, and they were without heart, and after a while rode dejectedly away.

They watched them go. Shep was having his arm bandaged. It wasn't much use now, but he didn't seem out of spirits.

'We licked 'em,' he was saying to his boss, and his voice sounded both pleased and surprised. 'Doggone it ef we didn't give them fellars the hidin' o' their lives!'

When he saw the last of the Awker men go trailing away along the dusty track, Iron Jack sighed and sank back on to the step of the cabin. He was caked in dust and sweat; he'd lost his hat and was sore from his two falls on top of the previous night's bruises. And his trouser leg was wet with blood from his wounded leg.

The Babe came out with a bucket of water and some liniment that he used on horses. He said it was good for humans, too, and it probably was, though it made Iron Jack yelp a few times when it burnt into his raw flesh. The out-riders thought it was funny to see the boss being put through it, and stood around and said admiring things about the Babe's medicinal knowledge. Everyone was in a roaring good mood, even, the big boss realized, Jack Irons himself.

The mail had gone through, and they'd dealt heavy punishment to their enemy, without suffering much damage themselves. It was something to be proud about, something to enthuse over – sufficient reason for their exhilaration now.

When he saw that the enemy had been driven off, Irons limped across to his own black stallion that the Babe had saddled ready for him, and gave the order to mount. He was leaving six men in the way station until the teamsters walked in to take over. From now on he intended to put an armed guard all through these badlands, so that no other ambush could be prepared for the mail riders.

Shep took a spare horse, and the party of seven men trotted easily back towards the town. When they were a few miles along the trail, they ran into the teamsters. There were around a couple of dozen of them, heading in this direction, and they told him a similar number had taken the trail east out of the town, to watch the desert trail beyond.

They were in a bad temper, hot and sticky from their long walk, and when they learned that they had just missed an exciting fight they didn't look any more pleased.

Irons told them that horses would be coming in within the next day or so from Carson City, and said when they did arrive a dozen of them should ride on and camp out at the way station beyond the Tahoe Range. This meant that he would have around thirty men to keep watch along this dangerous twenty-mile stretch of badlands. It was a tough job, even for so many men, but he thought, looking at them, they'd be tough enough to hold it down. He felt sorry for any Awker's men who fell into their hands in their present mood.

Teamsters just naturally hated walking!

They parted, and Iron Jack and his out-riders rode on. They came to Virginia City late in the afternoon, when the sun was low but still hot over those Tahoe Mountains they had just left. The town was quiet, as if storing up energy for the wild scenes that came with every night's darkness.

As he came into the town, Iron Jack's pulse was beating faster. If the Butterfield Stage had run to time, then Ann must already be here.

He saw an old woman with a shiny new frying pan, wearily climbing up a hilly path to a crude wickiup, and he called, 'Has the Butterfield bin in yet, ma'am?'

She straightened her weary back and looked down into his brown, eager face. He saw her nod. 'It sure, did. Came in from Austin a coupla hours ago.'

Iron Jack had hardly time to thank her before he spurred on his horse at a gallop to where the Butterfield freight and passenger office was. He thought he'd find her waiting there.

He swung off his horse, waving adieu to his men who went on to the wagon camp at Crooked Ford. When he got on to his feet he realized that he was so stiff he could hardly walk, and he had to drag himself up on to the raised boardwalk, step at a time. He went into the shadowy, dusty office. She wasn't on any of the chairs inside.

A frowsy old bum, who was too lazy to bend his back to try and make a fortune, came gaping at him from a back room.

Irons asked, 'You the clerk?' He wasn't sure. Few men stayed long at a clerking job when there was all the mineral wealth around to set their minds ablaze with desire.

But the fellow nodded, so Irons asked, 'I'm lookin' fer a Miss Ann Caudry. She was supposed ter come in with the afternoon Butterfield from Austin an' Salt Lake City.'

The bum ran a dirty finger over the toothless gums in his frowsy old head. 'Yeah, yeah,' he mumbled. ' 'Member the gal. Swell looker . . .' His voice mumbled off.

Impatiently, 'OK – where is she? I'm lookin' fer her.'

The bum looked vacantly out through a cobwebby window and considered. Then he remembered. 'Yeah, now I 'member. Me, I got a good memory,' he boasted. 'She got off'n the stage an' a fellar was right thar with his hat off an' sparkin' up to her nicely.'

'Someone to meet her?' Irons asked quickly. 'Who was it?' The bum shook his dreary head. 'What did he look like – where did they go?'

'He was just a fellar,' the clerk said vaguely. 'Yeah, just a fellar like you 'n me. There's hundreds around here jes' like him, I reckon.' He thought hard but couldn't think of any unusual feature in the man's

87

appearance to discuss. He went on, 'He got her luggage an' slung it on a two-hoss buggy, then helped her up an' drove off with her, but I don't know where. Mebbe someone up by The Sky's The Limit might know, mister.'

Iron Jack turned to go. He was disturbed. Someone had been in Virginia City to meet her, apparently, yet only he knew that she was arriving that day . . . .

Suddenly he remembered that letter that had been torn away with his pocket in the fight the previous night . . . he thought, 'That could have bin picked up an' read.' At once his pulse began clamouring; he felt something like a panic well up inside him.

For it could only be an enemy – his or the girl's – who could have found that letter and acted on the information inside it and not let him, Iron Jack, know of his intentions.

He went outside, and he felt so stiff and sore that he had to sit down on a paintless, rickety chair set out on the sidewalk. The bum came to the door. He was probably looking for a dollar and racking his brains to earn it. Iron Jack had his mind on other things than dollars and bums who didn't work for them.

He sat in the shade and looked at his horse, then looked down the wide street with its unlovely straggle of wooden achitecture. It looked desolate and dreary. Everything looked dreary. Even the sun seemed grey and lack-lustre.

For that's how a man feels when the girl he loves is in danger, and Iron Jack knew that she was in danger right now – knew it, and he didn't even know where to begin to look for her.

He heard the bum's uncertain voice. The fellow was working hard for a dollar, because a dollar brought a fellow a peg of whiskey, even out there in Virginia City.

The slurring, slovenly words trickled out through those gummy jaws. 'I figger you don't feel kinda pleased with what I told you.' Pause. ' 'T'ain't my fault, mister.' He wasn't getting anywhere. Iron Jack was just sitting and looking and trying desperatelv to think. So the bum said, 'That wasn't his buggy, though – that fellar that came an' picked up the gal.'

Irons lifted weary eyes. 'What do you mean, fellar?'

'What I say. He didn't own it, that buggy.' His dirty finger was exploring his toothless mouth again. 'I seed that buggy come in town two-three days ago, then again this mornin'. The fellar that was drivin' it then was a big, smart fellar. Nigh on as big as you, mister, but he'd got beef on his shoulders an' round his haunches. Yeah, I figger he's the fellar that owns that buggy. The fellar that met the gal he didn't look to own anythin' more'n I own, I reckon.' He ended with the contempt of one failure for another.

Irons stood up slowly, his face tight with suppressed fury. 'You tell me more about this big, smart fellar, brother, an' tell it quick or I'll knock all your teeth back into your head.'

The clerk blinked. He thought back, dismally, then brightened. 'Yeah, yeah, he looked like a gamblin' man. He wore a nice white shirt, an' a good suit o' black on his back. He'd got money, that fellar, anyone could see. But he would have, ef he was a gamblin' man. He had a big face that kinda grinned a lot, now I 'member, with a long black 'tache across it. Made him look like a cat, kind of . . . .'

Iron Jack was looking into space. He could see that face now; he knew it from the description.

It was the face of the most ruthless, the most conscienceless man he knew – Rolly Weyte.

Rolly Weyte wasn't a gambler any more. He owned three claims in the Sacramento Valley, though how he'd got to own them was the source of a lot of uneasy whispers around the coast. Weyte had money, now – more than he'd ever had in his life before. But he wasn't safe, and he knew it.

One man knew a secret of his; a secret that could get him hanged or shot. That man was Jack Irons, the outlaw wanted for murder in his native State of Kansas, but who was now operating as Pacific Coast boss for the big Russell, Majors & Waddell outfit.

Irons didn't dare show himself openly back in Kansas State, because there was bitter hatred against him – in this rough and ready West there was yet one thing that few men could forgive, and that was the slaying of a woman.

And that was the charge on those tattered bills that bore Irons' name seventeen hundred miles east of him. 'Wanted for the brutal murder of Belle Storr . . . .' That's what they said.

Only big Jack Irons hadn't done it, couldn't have done it. He wasn't the kind to harm any girl.

Still, he'd had to go on the run, had moved into other States where the Kansas peace officers had no power to operate and he was safe except for bounty men and avenging citizens bearing the justice of Judge Colt.

He'd run into Weyte the time he'd first met bonny Ann Caudry, niece of the man who had inspired this mind-gripping experiment, the trans-Continental Pony Express. Weyte had shaved off a beard, but he'd recognized him as the lover of poor Belle Storr – a man who had loved wherever there was money, but brutally left his infatuated women when the money was in his own pocket.

They'd brushed, and then Weyte had tried to kill him, and then Irons understood it all. Weyte had killed the girl because she was so much in love with him that she had intended to follow him, and he didn't want that. He'd killed her to rid himself of her – a brutal, appalling thing to do; he'd slipped away, leaving Jack Irons to take the blame because he'd been last seen with the girl. And when Irons had turned up in California he'd thought that Irons was trailing him for revenge. So, true to character, Weyte had gone out to silence the man he feared.

Irons had lost contact with his enemy since the days of preparing for the Pony Express. Now it seemed that Weyte had turned up here, in Virginia City.

Under his bronze skin Irons was pale. He was realizing that Ann Caudry, whom Weyte wanted but couldn't win, was now apparently in his enemy's power. It wasn't nice to think of that girl in the hands of the murderer of poor Belle Storr . . . .

Irons snarled, 'Any idea where that buggy comes from?'

The bum's eyes shot wide open at the tone. He went back a step, shuffling in the boots that he couldn't be bothered to tie up. He quavered in weak protest, 'Mister, I ain't got nothin' to do with that fellar. Me, I'm just a clerk aroun' here.'

Irons pulled himself together. 'Sure, sure,' he said quickly. It had got nothing to do with this hobo. He gave him the dollar, and the slouch looked grieved because he'd found that that way in this rich West he could sometimes get more. But he didn't get it from big Jack Irons.

The former Ranger and cow-wrangler limped down to his horse. This was no time to have a wounded leg, he thought savagely, but he had one, so he just had to try to forget it. It took some doing, because what the Babe had put on – that horse liniment – seemed to have made hot blisters on his flesh. Somehow, though, he got into the saddle, the sweat breaking out on his brow at the exertion and pain.

He rode a few yards down the street, then, without descending from his horse, bought a new seven-shot Sharps repeater to replace the one he'd dropped when Shep Clayton came plunging out to rescue him along the trail.

That done, he rode as hard as his bruised and wounded condition would allow, rode right into the big wagon camp at Crooked Ford. The men were sprawling around, resting after the labours of the trail and two nights without much sleep. They looked up as they saw the big boss come riding in. He was grey-yellow from head to foot from his hard-riding and tumbles on the trail; his face was strained and hard under the bruises and sores that marred it; and he rode like a man who has been too long in the saddle and it was time he got off and rested.

But Iron Jack wouldn't get down. For one thing, he felt that if he came out of that saddle he wouldn't ever be able to get back into it again, and he wouldn't give in while Ann Caudry was in danger.

He shouted for Thompson, and the wagonmaster was discovered with the blacksmith, attending to some broken wagon links. Iron Jack wearily rode over to him. Thompson looked concerned when he saw the big boss's appearance. 'Looks like you've bin through it more'n somewhat, Jack,' he said shortly.

Irons nodded. 'A bit,' he admitted. 'Look, Tommy, I reckon I've got need of your men agen. There's a gal I was aimin' ter meet from the Butterfield Stage today – she was met instead by a man who's workin', I figger, fer the doggondest skunk this or any other side of the Sierras, a fellar she loathes like anyone would loathe a poisonous rattlesnake. He's got her, an' I've got ter go out an' get her back.'

Thompson asked, abruptly, 'You know where he's taken her?'

'I c'n only think of one place – Awker's camp. Weyte – the fellar I'm talkin' about – knows Awker, an' once they looked as thick as thieves.' He considered, remembering what he'd heard about a 'gamblin' man' recruiting for Awker up the rough sea coast of California. It looked as though that was Rolly Weyte; so Weyte might have come in with the very bunch that had tried to lay for the pony rider that day.

93

'Yeah, I reckon we'll find Weyte up in Awker's camp,' he said. His head came up with some of his old fire. 'That gal mustn't stay in Weyte's power a minute longer than we c'n help, Tommy. I'm goin' in there to fetch her out.'

'What d'you want us ter do?'

'You follow up with all the men you can—'

'That'll take some time. We've only a few hosses, an' they're tired from today's travellin'.'

'That can't be helped. Bring up all your men as fast as you can; tell 'em about the gal, an' that'll make 'em fightin' mad, I reckon. I'm goin' in ter see what I c'n do. Ef I don't come out—'

Thompson looked at him from under grey, bushy eyebrows. 'Yeah?'

'Come in as fast as you can an' tear that Awker outfit ter pieces!' Irons' eyes were harder than the steel bits they used for the new rock-boring in the Comstock. 'Ef you can't do it yourself, send back into Virginie City an' let the vigilantes know there's a gal been took up agen her will into the Awker camp. You'll get the whole town with you.'

Thompson nodded. 'Sure, sure, Jack. I guess that'll bring 'em in the open agen the Awker toughies.' He glanced again at his boss. 'Why don't you wait, Jack, an' let us all march up together?'

Iron Jack pulled his horse round. He didn't want to sound heroic; he was too weary, too full of pain – and too anxious for the girl's safety to put on any pose. Instead he pointed to the dying sun and said, 'I've got to find her afore dark. Ef I don't, we'll never find her in the big Awker camp when it's night!'

He turned and sent his black stallion galloping

once more towards Virginia City. It was a race against the setting sun, and it was well that he had such a fine horse under him because the way was long and not too easy-going.

Awker had his wagon camp at a place known as The Fork. Here trails met from the northern lakes and the town of Sparks. It was north of Virginia City, on flatland between two ranges of high bluffs.

Iron Jack had often seen the camp in the earlier days when he was exploring the area to find the best track westwards for the Pony Express. It was a great, sprawling place covering several acres, with vast fenced-off yards in which were kept the mules, the horses and oxen used to pull the lumbering freight wagons over the mighty Sierras. The wagons were all drawn up in long rows at the south end of the camp, right alongside the fork where the trails met, and here was a little town of rough shanties, improvised by the teamsters, and tents, though many of the teamsters still slept in the wagons.

Because of the fear of thieves, and because there was little grazing now at The Fork, the valuable animals were always kept within the heavily-fenced yards, and a mounted guard rode night and day around the vast corrals. Iron Jack knew that to get into that hostile camp he must first evade the sentries.

He saw the Awker spread as he loped out on the trail towards The Fork, at a place where he could look down on to the plain between the high bluffs. The sun had almost set, and the last rays were a dying-red that tinctured the Awker camp with a bloody hue. Iron Jack found himself wondering if it was prophetic. If the angry Russell teamsters came storming into the Awker camp, it would certainly result in a mighty pitched battle.

Iron Jack paused to look down and thought, 'I've got to try an' get her out on my own.' If a brawl developed between the two outfits, the girl might get hurt; or, just as bad, Weyte might take advantage of the confusion to spirit her away to some other, unknown, hiding place.

Iron Jack didn't like to think of the suffering of the girl, now she was in the hands of the man she loathed and distrusted.

His eyes sought out a building that stood closest to the trail. This was used as an office by Awker, and Irons guessed that the boss also used it as sleeping quarters when in Virginia City. He looked at the office building, and he thought that he would find Weyte and Ann Caudry there.

Irons decided on that point, and then urged his horse down towards The Fork. He still had no plan. All he knew was that that setting sun dictated speed, and he couldn't sit back there on the trail and figure out pretty plans of rescue. He had to keep riding and hope that inspiration would come to him.

In fact inspiration wasn't required. He was still half a mile from the Awker camp when he saw a small group of horsemen come riding in from the West.

When he saw them the idea came to him that these men were probably riding in to tell Awker that his plan to stop the west-bound Pony Express rider had failed ignominiously.

They rode to the picket lines back of the office,

then crowded in through the front door. They weren't in more than a minute when they came out again, and Iron Jack could see, even from that distance, that they were an angry lot of men.

Awker came to the door after them. He had a bandage on his head. That would be from the fight the previous night inside the Silver Dollar saloon. Awker was shouting his head off after the men, and attracting attention all over the camp.

Still riding up, a solitary figure along that Virginia City trail, Iron Jack heard every word that Awker called his men.

According to Awker, he'd never met such a gutless, useless, worthless, no-good, chicken-hearted, lily-livered lot of cowards and weaklings in all his born days. The hell with 'em, they could get out of his camp! He wasn't paying men like them. One hundred men couldn't stop a single horseman! Awker became profane at that point.

The men went back round to their horses. Awker stumbled after them, still shouting. He seemed as stiff as Iron Jack was feeling right now. Awker shouted more insults, and at that the men turned and began to talk back to him. Iron Jack saw them all stand by the hitching rails and argue with Awker and grow heated in their arguments with the boss. He thought any moment they might get to blows, but they didn't.

While the camp, including the fence riders, was interested in the row, Iron Jack rode up to the front of the office. He left his horse out front with reins trailing, knowing that it would stand there where it was without straying.

He walked openly, boldly in by the open doorway. He was in a little passage. A door led off to his left; another to his right. There was a door at the end of the passage which could lead to yet another room or might give out on the back yard where the hitching rails were.

The door to his right was partly open. Iron Jack heard someone ask, peevishly, 'Who's there? Don't stand out there, come on in.'

He hadn't made any noise, entering, but perhaps his shadow had disturbed someone within. He froze in the passage, waiting for developments.

The door to his right swung a little on a current of air. Iron Jack looked through the gap by the hinges and saw a clerk within, working on some papers at a rough-topped trestle table. He looked annoyed, as if the row going on just behind the building was distracting to his work, and he was in a peevish humour, wanting to vent his spleen on someone for the interruption to his task.

He looked tough, for a clerk, with thick, hairy forearms under his rolled-up shirt sleeves, and a blue, unshaven jowl that was more appropriate to a miner than a man who lived by his pen.

He stopped work on his papers and looked hard at the door. He must have felt Iron Jack's presence there, and was suspicious because the intruder hadn't followed his invitation to "come on in".

Iron Jack had hoped that his suspicions would become lulled, and he would go back to his work, leaving him, Jack Irons, to explore through those other two doors. But with that row going on outside, the clerk probably thought it impossible to continue with his totalling, and he was keen to follow up any distraction himself.

Iron Jack heard a chair go scraping back, heard heavy feet thump across to the swinging door, and heard the clerk growling curses about 'goddamn' fools that didn't know to come in when they were told.'

The clerk pulled roughly back on the door, mouth opening to blast off a string of uncomplimentary adjectives at the lurker in the passage.

It was too bad. They were pretty original expressions, but they became lost to the world because that clerk all in a hurry changed his mind about what he was going to say.

For he saw a big, hard-looking *hombre*, trail-stained and with a face that was disfigured by cuts and bruises. And that *hombre* was standing so close to a big Colt revolver, it could have been his twin brother . . . and those grim, slitted grey eyes were a reflection of the grim, grey-blue lights that shone on the long six-shooter barrel.

The clerk changed his mind, and said, instead of his uncomplimentary words, 'Brother, you don't need that gun. Look, I ain't got no malice agen you!' And he shoved his arms skywards so rapidly that they nearly came unstuck at the sockets.

The clerk went back into the room as that big, grim man took a step forward. Iron Jack didn't show it, but he was in a frantic hurry – any time now that argument outside would end and Awker or someone else would return to the office. He wanted to be away with the girl, if she was in the building, before that happened, but first he had to dispose of this

99

rough-looking clerk.

Under his breath Irons was cursing the fellow. He couldn't afford this time spent in handling him. If only the clerk had gone out after Awker, leaving the building empty for the moment . . . But he hadn't.

Inside that bare, untidy office, with its one tiny window and rickety chairs and tables, Irons looked round desperately, seeking some way of disposing of the clerk. Then he saw a big case by the side of the round-bellied stove that hadn't been dismantled from the recent winter. Obviously the case was used for holding logs for fuel for the stove, though it was empty now. Iron Jack saw a lid to it, with a fastening to take a padlock, though there was no padlock attached at that moment.

He jerked his gun towards the case, said, 'Get in there, fellar – quick!'

The clerk's eyebrows jerked up. 'Me? In there?' His voice was incredulous. He'd have to fold himself inside it like a hedgehog going into its winter sleep.

Irons said, 'You – inside there,' and his tone was flat and there wasn't any arguing when he gave an order like that.

The clerk stepped into the box, hands still held aloft. He was uncertain, not liking this a bit. He didn't argue, for all that, because he didn't like the gun and he didn't like the *hombre* who held it. He was tough, but he wanted to go on living a little longer, and that combination facing him didn't augur well for a long life if he kept opening and shutting his mouth.

So he kept it closed, and reluctantly settled his limbs into the box. Iron Jack saw baleful eyes and a

100

blue-jowled face that was muttering silent obscenities at him. He bit off a few hard words of warning, because he didn't want an alarm to go up for a few minutes.

'Keep quiet, when I put the lid down on you. Ef you don't, I'll sure send a coupla rounds into this box, an' the splinters'll irritate you – ef the lead don't put an end to your need fer shavin'!' The clerk scowled at this reference to his scrub chin.

Then Iron Jack dropped the lid on him, and found a peg of wood to take the place of the padlock. He knew that if the clerk got his back up against the lid and heaved he'd get out of the box easily enough; but he relied upon his threat to keep the fellow inside and quiet long enough for him to search the building for Ann.

He didn't lose any time now, but raced back into the passage. The quarrelling was still going on outside, only it seemed to have shifted from the back and was beyond this room on the left of the passage.

He tip-toed along to that other door. Then his eyes fell on a big key sticking out of the lock. That meant that at least he could get inside easily.

Carefully he turned the door handle – he didn't even need to use that key; the door was unlocked and began to open. At once he felt a great disappointment. It was hardly likely that Ann would be held prisoner inside a room with an unlocked door. He thought, 'Where can she be?' He didn't know how he could search the rest of this great, sprawling camp before night came.

He let the door swing. This clearly was where Awker lived when he was at the Virginia City end of his business. There was a crude, wooden bed against the far wall, a tall chest of drawers and a cupboard in this part of the room that he could see. It was not too light inside now, as if the lingering rays of the departed sun couldn't find a way through a small cobwebby window.

Irons walked into the room. Why, he never knew. It looked empty enough.

But the moment he stepped beyond the door, he heard a gasp.

And that gasp came from Ann Caudry.

His head jerked round in astonishment. The girl was sitting, white-faced and frightened, on a chair by a table against the back wall. He saw her, saw her eyes wide open, registering astonishment, incredulous disbelief – and then joy, overwhelming and delirious. The pallor left her cheeks as hope brought the blood surging back into them. He saw her jump to her feet. She was wearing trail clothes of buckskin – a dull, tanned, red skirt and jacket over a pale blue silk blouse. Her soft, wavy hair was in some disorder, as if she had been struggling, but it looked rich and lovely and very feminine . . .

Rolly Weyte was on a chair right behind the door. He was sitting there, a big gambling man of a fellow, well-dressed, heavy and prosperous-looking, a big grin on his broad, cat-like face with its long black moustache. He had his gun out and pointing, though his first words showed that he didn't recognize the intruder.

Iron Jack heard his enemy drawl, 'You, fellar, what're you doin' bustin' into this room?'

Iron Jack faced round completely at that. His own

Colt was in his hand, but it was down at his side now because that apparently deserted room had fooled him. Weyte – the man who hated him because he feared him – had the drop on him.

And Weyte would have no compunction in killing him, Iron Jack knew.

# CHAPTER SEVEN

Afterwards big Iron Jack often reflected on life's ironies. His life was saved for him right then because of what Awker's bullies had done to him that night outside the Silver Dollar saloon.

They'd beaten his face so much that with its bruises and swellings he didn't look like the man that Rolly Weyte remembered Iron Jack to be. The girl recognized him, though Weyte didn't, for the moment – but then, a girl will recognize a man no matter how much he has been changed, if she cares for him sufficiently. And to Ann Caudry, there wasn't a man in the West to compare with this hard-riding, strong, resourceful, but ever kind and considerate Iron Jack. She'd ridden a trail stretching over sixteen hundred miles across the vast American continent, with only Iron Jack to protect her and hunt food for them both and fight against nature and two-legged enemies to get them through safely. Ann Caudry could never fail to identify him after that.

Big, heavy Rolly Weyte saw the girl jump to her feet in excitement, but he misinterpreted the move.

He grinned – he never seemed to lose that big, false, gambling man's smile – and said: 'This *hombre* won't do you no good, honey. For why? 'Cause he's gettin' to hell outa here right now!' His face still smiled, but his voice was a snarl. 'Beat it, brother!'

The gun waved towards the door. Plainly Weyte put him down as some teamster searching about for his boss. Iron Jack realized that the gun at his side must be hidden from Weyte's view, otherwise the big gold-mine owner from Sacramento wouldn't be treating him with such contempt.

So Iron Jack obediently turned and shambled towards the doorway. Then, just level with that gun hand that protruded in advance of the door, a sound came that brought Weyte jumping to his feet.

The row of arguing men seemed to have progressed towards the front of the office building, but the sound didn't come from them. It was a sudden, loud, snapping sound, followed by a mighty slam of wood against wood.

Weyte didn't know what it signified, but Jack Irons did.

The clerk was out of his box.

After a while in that cramped position, hearing no sound from inside that office, he must have taken a risk and heaved against the lid of the packing case. That snapping sound was the breaking of the wooden peg; the slam ... the lid flinging back against the side of the box.

Danger made big Jack Irons forget his sores and stiffness and the tiredness following the strain of long days in the saddle – the threat to this girl whom he had trailed quickened his thoughts and brought speed to his eager, gripping hands.

And Weyte didn't know who he was, so that he was offguard, anyway.

Irons, stepping back towards the doorway, flung himself sideways. His hands shot out almost as quick as light itself ... they grabbed on that gun hand, then Weyte felt the full weight of big Jack Irons falling on to his outstretched arm. No man could have withstood that leverage.

Weyte's arm was nearly jerked away from his body with the suddenness of that grip upon it. Then the leverage pulled the heavier man's body slamming hard down on to the floor.

Irons was turning in mid-air, even as he threw his opponent. He heard a suppressed cry of horror from the girl, then Weyte's body smashed face down on to the hard, unyielding floorboards. Irons rolled up on to his feet, and Weyte didn't have the gun now; it was in the former Ranger's lean, brown hand.

Weyte wasn't interested, anyway. He was stunned by the unexpectedness of that viciously swift wrestling throw. He could only lie on his face, hardly stirring, trying to pull his dazed wits together.

Irons grabbed at Ann. 'We've got to get out of here, quickly,' he panted. She hugged him; she was incapable of speech because she was nearly crying with relief at being in his arms again.

He pulled her through the doorway. The clerk was foraging around through some drawers. Irons thought 'He's looking fer a gun,' and began to rush down the passage.

Simultaneously two things registered on his consciousness. One was that he had to pass the open door of the room in which the clerk was; the second – that out front where his horse stood was a bad-tempered man named Awker in the midst of a crowd of followers.

Irons rocked back on to his heels right by that open doorway. If he'd gone another foot he would have stopped a bullet in his body.

The clerk had found his gun. There was no way of escape past that doorway now. Hearing the row out through the front door, Irons decided there was no sense in trying to escape that way, anyway.

He whirled. The shouting argument petered out as men realized there was shooting in the main office. Awker's voice came shouting angrily: 'What's goin' on in there, Bluey?'

The clerk's roaring voice filled the building with sound: 'There's a stick-up fellar in here, boss. I got him hazed up in the passage.'

Irons saw the girl's eyes, wide-open again with fear. He heard a groan from Weyte; then it seemed as though the big gambling man, who now owned three gold mines, was staggering to his feet.

Irons pulled the girl back to that third door at the end of the passage, just as he heard the sound of men's feet racing up to the door at the front of the office building.

The back door was locked, as Irons had guessed it would be.

He let fly with his Colt at short range, standing in front of the girl to protect her from any flying metal. Some wood splintered and splayed back on to his gun hand, bringing up a row of fine beads of blood.

The lock was hanging in a shattered plank of

wood. Irons lifted his foot and booted the door wide open.

He looked out on to hitching rails that were devoid of horseflesh, then looked beyond and saw acre after acre of high-fenced corrals with long straight runways between them.

On either side of him stretched the sprawl of shanties and wickiups and tents ... men were standing out before them, rough, brutal-looking Awker bullies, attracted by the noise across at the main office. There was no escape that way.

The front door burst open behind them, and Irons saw a throng of faces crowding into the passage. He lifted his Colt. He couldn't miss at that range. Then the hammer fell on an empty cylinder.

They didn't know it, that crowd in the doorway – didn't know that Irons had tried desperately to fire upon them and had failed because his gun was empty. They saw only the threat of that swift-lifting revolver, then they went tumbling backwards in mad haste to escape the hail of bullets that that ugly Colt promised.

Somehow the door swung to, leaving the passage empty. Irons took hold of the girl's hand and started to run with her across to the big pens. It was the only way of escape left open to them. They'd just got down a long alleyway that led between the high fences of some mule compounds when a shout went up behind them. Their way of escape had been spotted by Awker's men.

Irons saw a side alley that led between more compounds. These were filled with oxen, who turned to stare at them with bovine suspicion as they ran by. Irons found that the girl was running as easily – perhaps even easier – than he could himself, and he let go her hand, threw away the empty revolver that had been Weyte's, and drew out his own.

Again they came to cross alleys, and again they twisted away. Then more cross-alleys – more ducking and dodging down them. All around were horses, mules, donkeys, ponies and oxen, filling the air with low murmurs of unease as the pair went racing by. There was a stink of many sweaty, close-penned beasts, but neither gave any heed to such matters then. Smells weren't worth mentioning when a person's life was in danger, and they knew theirs were.

Back of them, men were running in among the maze of alleyways, searching for them, hunting them down. Irons thought: 'They'll have guns in their hands. They'll open up when they see me.' He'd get no mercy from this crowd, not with Awker and Weyte to encourage the men in their eager instinct to hunt him down and kill him. He, Jack Irons, had hurt this outfit too much recently for them to be forgiving.

In time Irons realized that he was lost. Not all these alleyways were straight or ran at right angles from each other. He had hoped to run right through and come out at the other side, but after a while he had a conviction that they were just running round among the many big pens and wouldn't ever come out into the open again except by accident.

So he stopped running. Now was the time for caution. It was no good running on and on, if that only brought them straight into the arms of their pursuers.

The light was bad. Irons stood the girl up by a huge baulk of timber, where she would be hidden from down the alley. He said: 'Don't you move, Ann. We've got to hold 'em off fer another five or ten minutes. Then we might escape in the dark across through these pens.'

He was remembering the last time he had tried to escape through a corral full of cattle. That had been in Kansas, at the headquarters of the big Russel, Majors and Waddell outfit.

His enemies had stampeded the cattle, so that he had been almost trampled to death under their sharp hoofs in the middle of that mighty pen. He didn't know whether he would risk taking the girl in among these oxen, because the same thing might happen again, and he shuddered to think of the girl going down beneath a sea of tossing horns . . . .

He stood behind a big fence-support, across the alley from her. That was so that if it came to gun-play, he'd be the target and would be attracting the bullets away from her.

Behind him a hundred draught oxen turned to look at him, every one with their heads held low, their big, mournful eyes dully apprehensive and filled with bovine suspicion. Iron Jack realized that every beast in that pen was betraying him to the enemy; every ox there was pointing towards him almost as if it were a finger indicating the way to the Awker mob.

But the Awker men weren't up with him yet. He could hear voices from several places in the corrals, some on either side of him, some seemingly just ahead. He tried to peer through the latticework of cross-beams that made up the many corral fences, but always there was some obstruction to restrict his range of vision.

Ann whispered: 'Can you see them?'

'Nope.' His eyes were grimly watching up and down the alley. He was crouching slightly, both hands filled with Colt revolvers. If he was stiff and sore now, he didn't notice it – imminent death got you forgetful of such trifles.

He heard her whisper: 'I knew you'd come and get me away from Weyte. You always do turn up when I need you, don't you, Jack?'

He heard her, yet he wasn't really listening. He was looking through the maze of supports and cross-poles; he had seen a movement of colour, as of someone's shirt. There was still that amount of light left for him to see.

And that shirt was lifting, as if the owner was climbing to the top rung of the corral so as to be able to look out along the alleys.

Ann was whispering: 'He said you couldn't meet me, Jack, and that he had to take me to your camp. I didn't know any better, and I got on to that carriage and went up to that dreadful place. I walked inside, expecting to meet you, but there was only Jud Awker there – and Rolly Weyte!'

Watching that head mounting against the evening sky, now a dull, purple-black within minutes of night, Irons thought: 'That fellar Weyte always goes out fer what he wants.' And the more he was repulsed, the more he strove to get what his mind was set on. He was that kind of man. The fact that Ann Caudry didn't want him made her all the

111

more desirable as a prize, and he'd shown that he was willing to go to any lengths to get her.

He called softly: 'Quiet, Ann,' and at the same time lifted his revolver to cover that rising, hunched figure above the corral. Above the lowing of cattle he heard men's voices right behind him, as if they were working down a parallel alley.

He didn't fire. He didn't want to bring the men all crowding down on to him. Another few minutes and he might find escape under the cover of darkness. Already it was difficult to see.

He clung back behind that supporting post, but he knew he wasn't completely hidden by it. He stood a good chance of escaping observation though, he thought; there was a lot to look at from that position on the corral rails before the searcher's eyes alighted on him. And every minute – every second – that passed was in his favour.

His eye just around the edge of that post, he saw the big, shadowy man clinging to the top rail and looking down along the alleys. It seemed that that face under the hat was turned to look along this alley . . .

The watcher snapped up with a gun and ripped off and Iron Jack knew that he had been seen.

He triggered lead even before he heard the thunk-thunk of bullets smacking into the beams before him, and he either hit the Awker man or his shot was so close that it made him tumble off the fence in alarm. The bulky figure disappeared. Jack Irons heard a shout of pain, and then there was a second of silence.

Then it seemed that everywhere around him he

heard running feet. The Awker mob was closing in on them. They were trapped.

Awker himself could be heard shouting orders in the distance. He was bellowing to the men to get around and cut off every alleyway. Then Irons heard a shout: 'Thar's five hundred bucks fer the fellar that brings Iron Jack to me – dead! I don't want to see him any other way.'

Iron Jack smiled grimly in the darkness. That was the kind of thing vicious little Jud Awker would say. He heard the swift rush of feet and then Ann was at his side. She whispered: 'I heard, Jack. Oh, Jack, it's my fault. I'm going down to speak with those men—'

'Ter plead fer my life?' Iron Jack laughed shortly. He had no illusions on that score. 'Spare yourself the trouble, honey. Even ef they promised, I wouldn't give myself into their hands. Awker's promise wouldn't be worth the rattle from a rattlesnake's tail.'

But he put his arm round the girl, all the same, and it felt good to hold her . . .

Then he noticed the poles that slipped across to form a gate in the nearest ox pen. It was getting so dark that the cattle within were just huge, shapeless dark masses now, relieved by the occasional white of uneasy, rolling eyes.

He whispered: 'Stand back agen the pen, Ann. We're not licked yet!'

There was a curious silence over the pens now. Even the cattle seemed uneasily quiet. Then Iron Jack heard a footfall along from him, and knew that the enemy was sneaking stealthily down this alley towards them.

He pulled out the bars, working as silently as possible. When the gate was made in the fence, he ran in and chased out half-a-dozen startled animals.

They came blundering into the alley, saw Ann shrinking against the fence, and shied and went loping dismally away from her. Irons came running out with them. He knew what would happen now. Other beasts were unable to restrain their curiosity about the open gateway, and anyway they had the example of their brothers and sisters, now loping away into the freedom of the night.

They came streaming out in a brown surging mass into the alleyway. When a few dozen had trotted off after the leaders, Irons jumped out and sent the rest milling the opposite way along the alley.

It gave him inspiration. He jumped across and pulled back the bars on the next pen; raced along and did it to another. In a few moments there would be hundreds of beasts racing up and down the alleys, and that would be confusing to the men – with all this movement around them they wouldn't so easily spot Irons and the girl in the near-darkness.

Irons grabbed Ann by the hand and ran her into the empty pen. They scurried swiftly across, apprehensive of detection and shouts and then, perhaps, bullets.

There was plenty of shouting. Raging voices had tumbled to Irons' ruse; the night was suddenly a hideous medley of furious men's voices, and dismayed bellowings from cattle that found there was, after all, going to be little freedom for them among these alleyways.

114

Irons and the girl slipped out through the rails beyond, into another alleyway. He got the stink of mules, even without looking at what lay in a corral. Mules sure would take some handling in those narrow alleys, he thought, and began to work frantically to pull back the pole-bar gates. They came out with a wild rush and a kicking of wicked hoofs. There was bedlam now, with those beasts rampaging in the alleys, joining up with the cattle and leading them boldly past the men who would hold them back.

Suddenly Iron Jack realized that this mule pen was on the outside of the yards – through that far fence was the open plain.

He took the girl across at a run. They clambered out. There was just a little light left, and they saw a mounted man riding up from the shack town. It was Weyte. They must have wandered in a big circle to have come out so near to the men's quarters.

Weyte came racing up, guns flaming. He was probably aiming for Iron Jack all the time, not intending to hit the girl. But he was in a mood when he wasn't bothered if she did get a bullet intended for his enemy. Hatred was stronger in Rolly Weyte than love – and he'd loved many a woman in his time, but never had he hated a man like big Jack Irons.

Irons went tumbling back through the fence poles, shooting with both hands and sending Weyte pulling away out of range. He groaned to himself. This was downright rotten luck. They'd got out from the trap within the pens, just when the light had almost gone, only to have the bad luck to blunder

115

into the most vicious of their enemies.

The mighty roar of voices and animal sounds seemed to increase with those shots blasting off. Then they heard Weyte's voice, out in the darkness. They could just see him, and they knew by that that he would see them if they stepped out on to the open plain away from the screen of corral poles.

He was standing in his stirrups, roaring: 'Jud, Jud, get your men round here! They're holed up in the mule corral!'

Then Awker's voice, rising above every other sound: 'To hell with them beasts! Every man git across an' surround the mule pen!'

Again they heard men's feet running towards them. That reward of five hundred dollars put wings to a man's legs.

The mounted figure of Weyte seemed to fade swiftly. Night had come. It had arrived about three or four minutes too late. That darkness, earlier, would have enabled them to sneak away from the pens unobserved. It was rotten luck, big Iron Jack thought despairingly.

The night was suddenly black about them, but it didn't hold back the sounds. The pair lay on the outside of the corral poles now, hugging the ground in case of a wild shot.

They heard men's feet cautiously treading down the alleyway back across the mule pen; then it seemed that men were inside, creeping steadily across the open space towards them. Iron Jack lifted his gun, but then he realized the futility of opening fire. The round wouldn't likely find a target in that gloom, but the flame from his gun would betray his position to the enemy.

More men were outside with Weyte, and he could hear them creeping in. They were surrounded. Even the darkness didn't help now. Awker began to shout, giving instructions to the men to close up and narrow the gaps in their circle.

Lying with his ear to the ground, still warm from the day's sun, Irons could hear the tremors running through the hard-baked earth as men cautiously pulled themselves in closer. Those within the corral couldn't be far from the fence now, he thought. Then the fence pole back of them vibrated. That meant that someone had blundered unto it, perhaps a few yards away only.

He came up on to his knees, pressing the girl down flat on to the earth as he did so. He wanted her to be out of harm's way when the bullets started to fly. Then he rose stiffly upright, never making a sound. His face was hurting, and his muscles felt bruised again, following that short rest. But he knew there was nothing wrong with the fingers that wrapped around the triggers of his Colts.

He stood, crouching, guns wide apart, ready to go down fighting when he was spotted . . .

It wasn't so dark now. It seemed that either his eyes were getting used to the blackness, or it was getting lighter. He had never known anything like it, light to come so soon after nightfall.

But it was getting lighter. Yellow light. Then orange. Now, suddenly, in one moment, it seemed, the world was bathed in a leaping red light.

He heard startled oaths from all around him, and the creeping stopped. He whirled. There was a red glow over the pens behind him. Awker was shouting, and never had he seemed in such a fury.

The animals were frightened and bellowing their heads off and running round in their pens and creating hell with their hoofs on the corral poles. Men were shouting all around him.

Ann's whispered voice: 'What is it, Jack?'

He crouched down beside her so as not to stand revealed against that growing light. He could see her face now, the light was becoming so bright.

'There's a fire.' His mind was working rapidly, trying to assess this situation in relation to their own danger. 'Looks like the office buildin' an' the shanties are on fire.'

All around them men were running. They'd got the same idea – that their shanties were on fire and their property was being destroyed. Iron Jack thought: 'This is goin' ter be mighty lucky fer us, this fire.' His pulse was beating rapidly. This diversion might draw off the enemy and help them to escape.

Awker suddenly began to roar instructions again. His voice was further away, as if he had run down towards the fire. They got his words in drifts. '. . . get that fire out . . . every man down here . . . .' And then: 'Drive 'em away . . . *it's Irons' crowd* . . . .'

Hearing the raging fury of that voice from the little freight hauler, Jack Irons suddenly understood.

He jumped to his feet, pulling Ann up with him. He exclaimed: 'It's Thompson! He must have arrived with the men ter find the Awker camp deserted!'

He didn't think Thompson would have ordered the place to be set on fire, but he knew those rough teamsters of his; knew they would be thirsting for revenge after the happenings on the desert outside Virginia City. Some of the wilder men would have started to burn down the office, as a gesture; then others would have started firing the flimsy, inflammable shacks and lean-to's.

They turned and looked over the pattern of interlaced corral poles that were silhouetted against the red fire to the east of them. Showers of sparks were flying hundreds of feet into the air as roaring draughts carried them up out of the blazing ruins.

Then, above the roaring of the flames, they began to hear the swelling tumult of men shouting in anger. Down there where the fire raged was the biggest brawl in years, with the men of the two outfits clashing in the light of the blazing camp. It was a pitched battle between two almost equally balanced armies of men.

Four hundred men locked in hand to hand combat, fighting in among the blazing cabins, rolling into the corrals under the feet of terrified, stamping horses. Sometimes guns were used, but mostly the fight was at too-close quarters, and sticks were swinging, and big, solid fists clenching and smiting.

Men were rolling on the floor in agony, and being trodden on by the fighters swaying on top of them. In time men didn't know who was who, and they hit out indiscriminately at any face or body that was within range. It was a bloody shambles of a battle, and the red glow from the hundred-feet-high flames only made it look the more sanguinary.

Jack Irons looked round and saw no enemy. He thought of his horse, that fine black stallion.

Thought: 'Mebbe Tommy recognized it, standin' there. He'll have it now with his own.' So he decided to go down, skirting the fight, to find the horses.

They broke away from the shadows of the high fencing, running together. Ann ran easily, because she was fit and not tired and sore as he was.

They came out into the open. The light was stronger here, and lit up the countryside for hundreds of yards around. They saw from this distance the fantastic spectacle of men embroiled in battle, silhouetted against the leaping flames of the shanty town.

The roaring of the fire drowned every other noise now. So it must have been instinct that made Iron Jack's head suddenly whip round, searching behind them.

He saw, within feet of him, a horse charging flat out at his back. Saw a gun pointing straight at him.

Saw a big, broad, cat-like face, grinning maliciously under a long, black moustache.

Weyte had been lurking in the distance, waiting for just this moment. The mice had come out into the open – now the cat was on top of them.

Iron Jack threw Ann away to one side, then fell down right under the hoofs of the charging horse.

# CHAPTER EIGHT

There wasn't time for him to do anything else. Ann was thrown safely clear in that movement, but he was off balance as a result of it, and could only go down on his face.

A bullet kicked up dirt at him as he dropped . . . his quick movement had, at least, spoiled that aim.

Then the horse leapt and cleared his form, as he had known it would. No horse will ever deliberately step on to an obstacle whilst running.

Iron Jack heard Ann scream, then felt the shadow of the beast cross over him. Another bullet ripped down at him as Weyte rode over his sprawling body, but that, too, missed.

The big boss rolled on to his knees, guns up and blazing. Weyte was racing his mount like fury towards the cover of darkness, was swaying in the saddle so as to present a difficult target.

But Iron Jack got him. It didn't bring Weyte off his horse, but he saw the rider stiffen in the saddle, and there was a movement as if an arm had gone dead and the other had come across to hold it. Then Weyte was thundering away out of range and into the blackness of the surrounding night.

Irons ran across to the girl, shouting: 'Run for it, Ann!' If Weyte had a rifle in his saddle boot, he might pull round and pick them off from a distance.

They ran towards the fire. The fighting was still going on, but Irons was looking not at the fighters but for the horses. His first concern was to get the girl safely out of this shambles.

He saw the big mass of horseflesh across the fork where the two northern roads met. Men were having to hold them, because they were frightened by the sounds of fighting and the roaring of flames.

Iron Jack ran the girl up towards them. The first man he recognized was old Marty, the old-timer. Marty's face lit up when he saw them both.

'Goldarn it,' Irons heard him say, 'the boys sure are takin' this place ter pieces jes' to find you – an' here you are!'

Irons looked at the other men holding the horses. There were enough to look after Marty's charges as well, he thought. So he said: 'Marty, I want you to take Miss Caudry back to Crooked Ford pronto. Find my hoss an' take her on it. Hand over these mounts fer the other pickets to look after.'

One of the other men came forward at that, leading Irons' stallion. The big boss didn't want to risk the valuable beast's life near this ruckus, and he knew he'd be able to get a mount when all this fighting was over, so he lifted the girl up into the saddle and saw her ride away with Marty.

Then he went across to find Thompson and pull the men out of the fight. The Kansas outfit had had a good revenge on Awker's mob for what they had done to them back along the trail. This was going to set back Awker by a good few thousand dollars, and his outfit wouldn't be much good for haulage work for days to come.

He found Thompson and a group of men coming in from the stockyards. When they saw his tall, lean, familiar figure, they came running.

Middle-aged, grey-moustached George Thompson grabbed his hand. 'We've bin searchin' the place fer you!' he exclaimed.

'An' taking it apart ter find me,' big Jack Irons smiled. He was growing to like the wagonmaster.

'You got the gal?'

'She's goin' back ter Crooked Ford right now. Old Marty's lookin' after her.'

Irons looked round at the fighting. There'd be no victory for either side, because the opposing forces were too well-matched. He said, tiredly: 'Call 'em off, Tommy. Let's get back ter camp.' He'd had enough of fighting; now he wanted to stretch his limbs on a bed somewhere and go to sleep for a fortnight.

Thompson and his aides went running away down the tall corral fence, shouting orders. Irons saw their men begin to pull out of the fighting and straggle across in weary little groups towards where their horses were being held – those that had horses. The others would have to walk it back into the town, but that was nearer than Crooked Ford, and they'd have recovered their strength by the time they got there and would probably celebrate the day fittingly.

And when he thought back to it, it was quite a day to celebrate, Irons thought. They'd defeated the ambushers out in the Tahoe Hills, had thwarted Rolly Weyte's kidnapping scheme, and this night had done as much damage to the Awker outfit as Awker's men had done to the Kansas company three or four nights back.

He was walking head down, exhausted, along with two or three of his men. They were approaching the horses from along the lakes' road, and were away from the glow of the raging fires.

Irons heard the footsteps of his companions quicken and come up around him. He lifted his head. There were three men. They were looking at him. One of them stepped behind him. He started to turn, wondering at the way they looked at him.

Then his head blew up. Something crashed on to his skull and he sagged and went down, and the cascade of sparks as his consciousness faded was like the dying flare from the Awker office building as it finally collapsed inwards on itself and began to burn out.

Ann was first to begin to worry over Irons' absence. She was standing within the wagon ring, by one of the big fires that the cooks had got going against the return of the weary fighters.

As the out-riders, led by Thompson, came cantering in, she ran forward, trying to identify the big ex-Ranger among them. He wasn't there. She saw that each horse was doubly laden with wounded, some of them lying across the saddle bows, and she went round, looking at them with dread in her heart in case she found him among them.

But he wasn't there.

She saw Thompson, dismounting with the deliberation that his years demanded, and she went hastily across to him. He saw her face beginning to get concerned, because she had expected to find Irons in first with the returning horsemen.

Unfortunately Thompson got things a bit wrong and temporarily wiped away her fears.

She said: 'Where's Mr Irons?'

Thompson removed his hat. This would be Ann Caudry, the girl over whom all the trouble had been. He didn't blame Jack Irons for wanting to move heaven and earth to get her away from the clutches of Rolly Weyte, by what he'd heard of the man. This girl was as lovely as any he'd ever seen – a fine-looking, intelligent girl.

Thompson smiled gallantly. 'You're Miss Caudry, I guess?' She nodded. 'Jack Irons?' He looked vaguely round. 'He's somewhere aroun' the camp,' he assured her. 'He rode in ahead of us.'

Then he shouted to a couple of wranglers to go round the wagon ring calling for the big boss.

Thompson had to go away to attend to the wounded, and the girl went back to the fire where a heavy-fisted cook shoved a great pot of scalding coffee into her hand.

She felt easier now, following Thompson's reassurance, and stood and talked to the cook and drank his coffee. Other men came up, and they all stood in a chatting group.

But still Jack Irons didn't arrive.

The two out-riders came back from the lines, reporting that Irons wasn't to be found. Ann spoke to them, feeling a little desperate, her instinct telling her that something had gone wrong with the big boss's plans.

'He must be about. That man I spoke to with the grey moustache—'

'That's Thompson, ma'am. You picked on the wagonmaster.'

'He said Mr Irons was already in camp some-where.' She looked at the mighty array of wagons. 'You must have missed him. Perhaps you didn't shout hard enough.'

'Ma'am,' said one of the out-riders politely, 'no one misses the kind of shoutin' we put up just now. Nope. I figger Iron Jack's not yet rode in.'

Thompson came over just then, and was given that report. He said shortly: 'Use your eyes an' you'll see the big boss must be here.'

He was pointing to a horse that was staked out inside the wagon circle, where the most valuable beasts were always kept. It was a mighty black stallion.

'That says the boss is back,' Thompson was saying, and then Ann became frantic. She caught his outstretched arm.

'No, it doesn't. Jack put me on his own horse – I came in on that, not Jack Irons.'

It was Thompson's turn to be flabbergasted. He hadn't thought of that.

Then Ann was saying, urgently: 'Something's happened to him. He was going to get a horse some-how, somewhere. He'd have been in by now if some-thing hadn't happened to him. *For something has happened to him!*'

She was suddenly frantic with worry, and all

around her the men were beginning to show concern, too. Thompson awoke into activity. He went striding around, getting the out-riders out of their blankets, questioning them and trying to find out who had last seen the big boss. In the end it seemed that he, Thompson, had been about the last man to see him down at the Awker corrals.

He was worried, but he tried not to show it to the girl, because he knew that her worry was greater. He strode back to her.

'No one seems to have seen him since the fight out at Awker's place.' He went on quickly: 'That don't mean anythin', of course. I figger he couldn't get a hoss, after all, an' he's havin' ter hoof it back through Virginie City with the other men. I'll send a coupla men in with a spare hoss ter try'n get him back before dawn.'

She tried to accept the theory, but it was a dismal effort. Instinct told her it wasn't sound. Iron Jack wasn't the kind of man to walk when he'd planned to get a horse from somewhere. He'd have got one, somehow, she was certain.

But there wasn't anything she could do about it. She saw two out-riders trot off along the winding trail into the town, and then she was led to a covered wagon which had been prepared to receive her.

There was a good soft bed in it, made up by the camp cooks. But she didn't sleep. She lay there hour after hour, listening and hoping for the sound of Jack Irons' deep, drawling voice.

But she hadn't heard it when the first streaks of grey light came filtering in through the weathered canvas roof over the wagon. And with the dawn, if she'd had any doubts before, she had none now. Now she knew that only some kind of disaster must have befallen the man she loved for him to be kept away so long. By now he could have walked the entire distance from the Awker camp, if he'd been forced to do it.

She got up and dressed and went to the fires. She was shivering, because the wind was up and it was raw from the coolness of the night.

Very few people were stirring. It turned out that most of the teamsters had stayed overnight in town, after painting the place a bright, jubilant red, following their smashing defeat of the Awker camp. A few men were moving stiff limbs across to get an early morning drink from bad-tempered cooks who always had to get up first, anyway.

Then George Thompson came stumping heavily across towards her, and the mere fact that he was already up and around confirmed her own fears. Thompson, too, was worrying; for all his words of reassurance, he didn't believe them himself.

He came uneasily across and said: 'Good-mornin', Miss Caudry.'

She said: 'Jack – he didn't come in?' She was worried stiff.

He sighed. 'Nope. He didn't come in. I watched up most o' the night, but he never showed up.' His eyes shot a quick glance at her, as if to estimate her capacity for taking bad news. 'Mebbe somethin' did happen to him, last night,' he said cautiously.

She wrung her hands in despair. 'I'm sure it did. It could have been so easy, with all those Awker men around.' And she wondered if perhaps it wasn't anything to do with Awker, but that he had run into vengeful Rolly Weyte, riding around in the darkness. Weyte mightn't have missed the next time he tried a treacherous attack.

She whispered: 'What can we do, Mr Thompson?'

And he said, tonelessly: 'I don't know what there is we can do, ma'am.'

They went across and got breakfast, then Thompson sent out all the out-riders he'd got to search the town for the big boss.

All during the morning reports began to trickle in to them at the big wagon camp at Crooked Ford. Men were streaming in from the town, weary after their night's celebration. They brought news that the Awker outfit had had to work throughout the night to beat out the fires that had been started, and now they were ranging the plains in search of the beasts that had got away from the corrals. By all accounts, from what the men had heard, the temper was murderous, up at the Awker headquarters.

Then in came the long-awaited horses from the Carson City stables. The out-riders who drove them reported that the trail was apparently clear – certainly no one had tried to molest them. They'd left a couple of dozen mounts at the last way station in the Tahoe range, to get some of the spare teamsters out to cover the pony trail as far as the second Tahoe way station.

The remaining horses should have been ridden out to the way station east of the town, where other teamsters were awaiting them, but acting on a hunch, George Thompson ordered them to be kept in the camp for the day. He had a feeling that, with the disappearance of the big boss, they might have sudden, urgent need of them here at Crooked Ford.

Then the out-riders came back, one by one reporting no success to their search. A couple of them had scouted all across the country as far as the Ford. They'd seen the Awker outfit still at work among the ruins of their camp, but nowhere did they see any sign of their boss.

The men were openly saying now that big Jack Irons must have run into some of the Awker men in the dark and been killed out of hand and his body buried where no one would ever find it. Thompson did his best to keep this speculation quiet, but in the end it got to Ann's ears and he saw that the thought terrified her. Terrified her because it was something that lay at the bottom of her own heart, that dreaded feeling of utter disaster.

About noon, when it became apparent that Jack Irons was not going to turn up, his men got together in a big, angry bunch. Thompson stood back from the meeting, because he knew these men weren't in the mood to listen to his habitual caution.

A big, hairy-chested teamster was up on a cart, shouting vengeance to the men. They were very much partisan now, these men from Kansas. They identified themselves with their boss in his present predicament, because the boss's enemies had been theirs, coming in.

Now loose talk of revenge fell on receptive ears. The big, hoarse-voiced teamster was urging the men to band together, to go across to the Awker camp again and this time not leave the place until they'd found their boss. The men roared their approval, in a vicious mood following their night's rioting and dissipation; they were ripe for any mischief.

Thompson stood by Ann and said, depressingly: 'This won't do no good. This time the Awker mob'll be ready for 'em, an' when the scrap's finished there won't be either an Awker mob or a Kansas outfit.' What he didn't say was that he considered the big boss to have been disposed of, and so it was useless going anywhere with thoughts of rescue now. They were too late.

They stood together, the girl off her head with anxiety, while the men ran across to their wagons and got their weapons ready for another sortie.

They never went out, though.

Three visitors came cantering up the trail to them. One was the sheriff. The others were his deputies.

Thompson went out to meet them. The sheriff was a man much like himself, middle-aged and wanting the comforts that should go with middle-age; grey-moustached, stocky and a little stooping.

But he didn't like the sheriff. The man was too plainly all out for himself.

He rode into the wagon ring, followed by his two deputies. He reined in, watching the activity as the men clambered over the tailboards and saw to rifles and revolvers.

When Thompson walked across he was greeted with a harsh – 'Where'd you think that army's goin', mister?'

Thompson looked coldly at the star on the sheriff's chest and said: 'I ain't got no thoughts about the matter. It's what they cooked up themselves. They're figgerin' on bustin' in a few people, I reckon.'

The sheriff leaned down from the saddle, frowning and trying to intimidate the wagonmaster. 'Looks like I came in time. Where c'n I find the boss?'

'I'm the boss,' snapped Thompson.

The sheriff gestured impatiently. 'I want ter see Jack Irons. He's the big boss, ain't he?'

So Thompson told him that Irons wasn't there, and he watched the sheriff closely while he spoke. Told him he hadn't been seen since the previous evening, and he didn't know when he would next be heard of.

The sheriff didn't notice the cautious way in which the wagonmaster phrased his speech, and at the end he broke in impatiently with: 'Wal, when he turns up, you tell him to come on in an' see me. There's bin a complaint laid against your outfit by Jud Awker. He rode in ter Virginie City this mornin' to tell me that your crowd had burnt him out. He's wantin' me to slap your boss behind bars—'

Thompson broke in quickly: 'Say that again.'

The sheriff looked surprised. 'Awker sure is mad against Irons. I've never seen a fellar madder. If he could lay hands on him, I figger he'd string your boss up so high, you'd see the soles of his boots.'

'An' he wants Jack Irons slapped into jail?' Thompson's eyes were narrowed.

'He sure does. He says he's gonna sue the Russell, Majors & Waddell firm fer fifty thousand dollars, an' he holds their representative, Jack Irons, responsible fer last night's outrage an' wants him brought fer trial afore a judge.'

'So you want ter see him to tell him all that?'

The sheriff got confidential. He leaned from his saddle and said: 'Look, fellar, I ain't got nothin' agen nobody, see? I ain't got nothin' agen your crowd at all. But when a prominent citizen like Jud Awker comes an' makes a charge, I gotta do somep'n about it, see? So you tell your boss ter ride over an' we'll hold pow-wow on the subject.' He gave a heavy wink at Thompson.

The wagonmaster's lip curled in contempt. He had no time for men who were paid to do a job but tried to ease their way through it by pandering to the people who were strong enough to put pressure on him. He could see that the sheriff didn't give a hang about justice, so long as he had a quiet life and continued to draw his comfortable sheriff's pay.

So Thompson, who was thinking of other things, said: 'I'll tell him.' But he didn't say that he didn't know when that would be. He was mystified by what the sheriff had told him. Ann came up and he whispered in her ear. She seemed bewildered, too.

The sheriff pulled round his horse to go. He was a crude, insensitive man. Right there in front of the girl he had to ask: 'That fellar Irons, your boss, he's wanted fer murder, ain't he? Fer killin' a gal back in Kansas.' He didn't notice the fury that mounted to Thompson's face at those words, or the anger that clouded Ann's fair countenance. He said: 'There's a tidy reward fer him in Kansas, I'm told – five hundred bucks. That's some money.'

Ann said: 'It's blood money. Most of it's been put up by Rolly Weyte. Jack Irons never hurt that girl—'

The sheriff's cold eyes swung dispassionately to regard her. He asked: 'How d'you know, ma'am?'

133

'Because Jack Irons told me he'd never killed her.'

'A fellar wouldn't admit to killin' a woman – not to another pretty gal,' the sheriff said brusquely.

'But I've been on the trail with him. I know him well. Once for weeks on end we rode together back to Kansas when he was trying to get this Pony Express started.' Ann faced him with defiance. 'No man could have behaved as he did, so thoughtful of my comfort, so concerned that I didn't get hurt – so fine, so gallant – and be the killer of a girl. I know it, Mister Sheriff. And I know who killed that girl – Jack Irons told me.'

The sheriff's rough voice was barely polite but a whole lot cynical. 'Who?'

'Rolly Weyte. He's responsible for three hundred dollars of that five hundred reward that's been offered for Jack Irons, dead or alive. He's made the reward attractive in the hope that Jack will swing for the crime he, Weyte, committed years ago. If Jack dies for it, then Weyte is safe. But whilever Jack is alive, Weyte is in danger, because some day his sins will catch up with him.'

The sheriff said: 'You may be right, ma'am,' but his tone was disbelieving.

Thompson came in on the conversation again. 'You know Weyte?'

'He was in my office a coupla hours ago.' His eyes lifted from sombre contemplation of the churned up earth.

'He came in with Awker on a buggy. The pair of 'em could hardly move fer sores an' stiffness, though that Weyte fellar was by far the worst. He'd been in ter see the doc afore he came in ter me. He laid charges agen your boss, too. Said he'd bust him on the head an' knocked him unconscious, then later shot him through the shoulder from the darkness.'

Ann said levelly: 'I can tell you a lot more about both incidents, Mister Sheriff. I was there both times. When I've got time I'm coming to you to lay charges against Rolly Weyte, too.' At the moment she had thoughts for nothing else but big Jack Irons and his safety. Weyte could be dealt with later – if this slippery sheriff was capable of dealing with anybody.

The sheriff opened his mouth, as if to try to talk her out of the idea. Then he saw Thompson's cold, contemptuous face and shut up hurriedly. He knew what was in the wagonmaster's mind, and he didn't want to hear Thompson's thoughts spoken bluntly aloud in front of his deputies. He saluted silently and then turned back down the trail to the town again.

Ann found herself deserted, immediately. She saw the wagonmaster go across to where the men were collecting. Thompson climbed on to the tail of a wagon and lifted both hands to get silence and attention.

Then he shouted: 'You're wastin' your time, fellars. You won't find the boss in the Awker camp. Instead you'll jes' get a lot o' lead blown at you, an' I'll be needin' new teamsters!' There was a savage roar at that, as the men shouted, the hell, they could blow lead back at the Awker mob, too, couldn't they?

Thompson got impatient and shouted to them to shut their faces.

'Awker an' his friend, Weyte, are in town right now, gunnin' fer the boss. Does that look like they've already got him or killed him?'

The crowd fell silent at his shouted words.

'I don't know what's happened to Iron Jack. I'm worried stiff about him. He should have come in by now, but one thing I feel certain about – the Awker mob don't know what's happened to him.'

'Then what has happened to him?' someone shouted, and at that Thompson could only lift up his hands helplessly. He couldn't even start to guess.

It left the men uncertain, and with uncertainty came indecision. In the end they broke up into little knots, all arguing, all theorizing – and all getting nowhere. Then they found they were very tired men, after all, and they got down to sleep.

Thompson went back to where Ann was standing with Shep Clayton. Shep had his wounded arm in a sling, but he was still in circulation and ready to ride wherever one sound gun hand might be required.

Shep said: 'That'll please you, Tommy,' jerking his head towards the retiring teamsters.

Thompson said, grimly: 'It's somethin' we might save out of the wreck, Shep. We're paid ter start a haulage business, not a war, an' the way we're goin' on we'll have neither men nor beasts left soon.'

Ann said, despairingly: 'But Jack – what about him? Where can he be? What can we do?' She was breaking under the agony of uncertainty.

Shep said: 'I'm goin' ter town,' and swung away for his horse.

Thompson and the girl went into town, too. It was

quiet, hot and dusty and they trailed about all day, always hoping, yet never getting a clue as to big Jack Irons' whereabouts.

At the Pony Express office the hostlers and the one mail clerk were warned to keep their ears open, in case there was anything to be heard regarding their boss. They were concerned when they were told of his disappearance, because Iron Jack was popular with them, and they promised to keep watch for him.

As the trio were leaving the office, the clerk said, doubtfully: 'Now, what's gonna happen to the west-bound mail tomorrow?'

They looked at him. They'd forgotten that tomorrow was Saturday, and if the mail ran to current speed it would pass through the town some time during the day – probably in the afternoon, was most people's bet.

Thompson shrugged. 'We've got men both ways along the trail. I figger it'll get through with them watchin'.' He wasn't interested in the mail; his concern was for the big boss upon whom depended the starting of this freight haulage business over the Sierras.

They rode back into camp. Iron Jack hadn't showed up. Now Ann was frantic with worry, and she spent another night without much sleep, starting up every time she heard a horseman enter the camp.

About noon the following day a rider came into sight along the trail, flogging his horse pretty hard. He rode across to the awning that had been put out from a wagon to provide shade against the blistering sun. Shep, Marty and the girl were there; then Thompson came across when he saw the lathered horse of the rider.

It was a hostler from the Virginia City rest station.

Thompson called: 'What's up? Anythin' wrong?' He wanted to ask: 'Has Irons turned up?' but he didn't want to sound too hopeful.

The hostler wiped the sweat from his hat-band. 'We don't know.' He was doubtful. 'A fellar slipped in ter tell us he'd got wind of a queer rumour.'

'Yes?' All four watched him intently.

'They're whisperin' around town that the rest station's gonna be held up an' the mails destroyed so's ter get the Pony Express in bad with the Federal Mails.'

Thompson's eyes flashed angrily. 'Oh, yeah?' he said. He turned to Shep. 'Get a dozen men ready ter take the trail pronto. We're gonna sit all around that office an' make sure no passel o' gunmen come an' get the mail.'

They all went for their horses. When they were mounted, they saw that Ann had got up on Jack Irons' stallion. They tried to dissuade her from accompanying them, but she wasn't going to stay back in that camp without them. Her nerves were on edge, and she craved for action of some kind.

They rode fast into Virginia City, in a swelling cloud of dust that coated them from head to foot and filled their eyes and got into their mouths and nostrils. But they weren't concerned about appearances. They thundered down to the rest station, where new riders took over the mails, wheeling in behind, where the stables were.

As they came into the office through the back way, they saw the clerk peering anxiously out through a front window.

Thompson shook the dust from his bandanna then wiped his face clean. He demanded: 'Everythin' all right?' The clerk came round then. He looked very uneasy. 'Come an' have a look at this,' he invited, 'only, don't let 'em see you're lookin'.'

They crowded to the window, but didn't grasp what the clerk was getting at.

He pointed. 'Look,' he said, 'ever seen so many people in Virginia City at this time o' day? Look, there's dozens o' men hangin' around.' And he turned on them and asked, shortly, 'Why?'

Ann peered over Thompson's shoulder. She saw little groups of men squatting on steps or standing against clapboard walls all the way up the street. They weren't doing anything in particular – just standing around, talking in desultory fashion, and drooping in the hot sunshine.

The clerk said, grimly: 'Fellars don't sit in the sun, not when there's a coupla dozen bars open.' He wagged a tobacco-stained finger to emphasize his words. 'An' them fellars look like teamsters ter me, an' I'd say they're Awker's men.'

'Then,' said Thompson, 'they're not hangin' around fer nothin'.'

He walked to the door and looked up and down the street. After a careful scrutiny he came back and reported: 'Looks like the hull darn' Awker mob's waitin' out there. Nigh on a coupla hundred of 'em strung up an' down the street.'

Someone asked: 'Waitin' fer what, Tommy?'

It wasn't a question that needed to be answered, not after the rumours that had gone around the town earlier.

'The mail, of course.' Thompson stuck his hat back on his head, as if that gesture denoted the start of action. 'Looks like they're determined ter stop the mail goin' through this time. They figger on grabbin' the rider as he comes down to this station.'

He looked at his dozen or so supporters. It had seemed enough when they set off; they hadn't thought of a holdup involving hundreds of men.

He ordered Shep to mount. Shep was wounded and better out of the way, anyway. He told him to get out on to the trail east of the town and wait for the Pony Express rider. 'Tell him ter give Virginia City a miss this trip an' go round the town to the Tahoe way station.' If no rider came into town, there'd be no trouble, and George Thompson didn't like trouble.

Shep climbed up and went racing out of town. Watching from the window, Thompson and Ann saw the loungers look hard at the rider, and there seemed to be a ripple of quick discussion among them.

'They guess there's somethin' afoot, but don't know what.' That was Thompson's opinion. They were relieved when the lone rider got through, all the same, for if he had been stopped they would have been in a bad position, trapped in the centre of the town.

Then they sat back to wait, though they didn't quite know what for. The minutes dragged by; the heat inside that wooden office was stifling, even though all doors and windows that could be opened were as wide as possible.

It was one of those windless, desert-hot days that left men weary and wilting and seeming without energy. Even the clock seemed affected by it, and the hands crawled round slower than Ann had ever known them to do.

The town lay broiling in the hot, summer sun, paintless, bleached grey by constant exposure to the fierce rays. Good citizens sat back in the shade and tried to sleep if they had no work to do, and even in the bars no one had the energy to call for a drink or lift a bottle to serve one.

But those loungers, lurking down the side streets, standing in doorways, and sitting on the raised boardwalks – they never moved. However uncomfortable it was, they stayed on. Cursing, no doubt, but staying . . . and waiting.

Then, all in one moment, everyone had energy. Suddenly weariness flew away along with boredom.

Suddenly the atmosphere in that town was electric.

A solitary rider had appeared at the end of the long, dusty, hot street. He came in fast, the dust kicking up in clouds under the feet of his fine, striding horse.

A ripple of sound passed like lightning down the street – they heard it even inside the office. A rough, growling roar: 'It's here – the Pony Express!'

Then the horseman came flying up to the office. He was almost unrecognizable, so clothed was he with trail dust. But Ann was thinking he was big for a Pony Express rider.

The Pony Express rider seemed to be stiff, seemed lame in one leg. He was bent double, as if badly hurt. But he grabbed the *mochila* and swung round.

And then, just at the moment when two hundred men began to storm towards the rest station, they saw that Pony Express rider's face.

It was big Iron Jack.

# CHAPTER NINE

When that unexpected blow fell on the big boss's head, he passed out for a good half-hour. When he came slowly to consciousness, it was to find himself slung across a horse in front of a rider, cantering through the night.

He felt bad, and moving made him groan and that told his captors that he was returning to consciousness. Someone growled a curse as he tried to pull himself upright, and a heavy hand flattened him once again across the warm, moving back of the horse.

He lay still, his head throbbing, his body on fire from his many sores, but all the while he was recovering, his strength was returning to him.

They seemed to ride on for hours, and then finally the men halted and got down. Iron Jack slipped off the horse, crumpling on to the ground as the muscles of his legs refused to support him.

Someone immediately slipped a rope round his ankles and then fastened his wrists behind him. Whoever it was wasn't gentle.

'You're not takin' any chances,' Iron Jack found

143

voice to say grimly.

A terse voice agreed. 'Not with a hide worth five hundred dollars, we ain't.'

A fire was lit and supper made. By the red glowing light Irons was able to see his captors. They were three rough-looking *hombres*. He knew them all by sight – teamsters who had come in with the long wagon train from Kansas.

They sat him up and released his hands so that he could have coffee. He didn't want anything to eat. While he was drinking, his captors sat across from him, their eyes alert and watching, ready for any sign of danger from the darkness around them and from their prisoner. Plainly they had a great respect for the big boss.

While he was drinking, Irons was thinking. At last he spoke.

'You're runnin' out on the outfit, huh?'

'Sure.' A big, sag-bellied teamster growled out the reply. 'An' why not? We didn't sign up ter fight a war. We reckon Kansas is the place fer us. Anybody c'n have Nevada!'

'You're goin' home, huh? Quittin'? An' you figger on takin' me back at the same time because I'll be worth five hundred bucks to you back in Kansas State?'

The big, heavy teamster nodded grimly. 'That hit on your head didn't stop your brain makin' good guesses.' But after that they wouldn't answer more questions. Instead they bound Iron Jack and then rolled themselves up in blankets and went to sleep.

The big boss never forgot that night. He was stiff and sore enough, but those bonds restricted the flow of blood to his limbs and most of the night he was in agony. Yet there must have been times for all that when he managed to fall asleep, for they had to waken him when dawn came and breakfast was ready.

All that day they rode, keeping off the trail because his captors weren't certain of the reception they'd get if they were seen with a prisoner. Bounty hunters weren't popular in the West in those days.

By late in the afternoon the three captors, if not their prisoner, were ragged in temper because of the strain of riding in the appalling desert heat. So, when they came suddenly, unexpectedly, upon a tiny prospector's cabin in a valley, surrounded by dense thorn scrub, they departed from their resolution to avoid people, and rode down in search of a cool drink.

The place was deserted. At once the natural greed of the men asserted itself. The big sag-belly looked quickly round, then said: 'Mebbe he's struck somethin', this fellar.'

The three men looked at each other. 'Yeah, mebbe he has. Lots of these desert rats scrape together quite a bit of gold,' another of them said quickly. He looked in at that single-roomed cabin made from wagon wood salved from the nearby trail. 'I guess ef he's got any, he's hidden it in there.'

The men slipped from their saddles, forgetting caution in their avarice. If they could find a poke of miner's gold, that would make this trip back east doubly profitable. They began to run into the cabin, and then the big sag-belly remembered.

He turned and looked at Irons, sitting alone up on

a horse. Irons saw grim, slitted eyes under shaggy, dust-powdered brows; he saw a face that was threatening and evil, and a rifle that lifted in a big fist as though it was a toy.

The leader of the trio called: 'Hold hard, there. Somebody stay outside an' keep watch. Ef we don't, five hundred dollars'll jes' ride away. Yeah, an' mebbe the desert rat'll come walkin' in on us.'

They left one of their number standing outside on guard. He had his rifle ready, so that any attempt to spur away his horse would have resulted only in a bullet speeding into his body, so wisely big Jack Irons sat there and didn't make an incautious move. He was bred to the philosophy of the West – that while there was life there was always a chance for a man.

He heard the men drink in turns from a tall Mexican earthenware bottle that kept water, even here in the desert, at near-zero temperature. It was handed out to the man on watch, but he didn't offer any to their prisoner, though Irons' mouth was so dry now that he could hear his tongue rasping when it moved inside his head.

Then the sag-belly and his partner began a systematic search of the cabin. Having begun, they went at it boldly, determined to get any gold that was there, and unheeding of the damage they did in their swift and ruthless search. They even got a spade and began to turn over the soft earth floor.

Suddenly Irons heard a new sound. From his position up on the saddle he could see over the top of much of the thorn scrub. He saw movement – saw someone walking wearily down towards the cabin.

He guessed it would be the prospector – and guessed that the man would walk innocently in among them, not knowing they were there until he was covered by that rifle.

So suddenly Irons exploded into sound. 'Goddamnit, get that gold quickly, can't you, an' let's beat it outa here! It's so hot, I can't stand it!'

He shouted the words, like a man giving way to blind anger, and he saw the oncoming prospector halt, back there in the scrub, and knew that his warning had got through.

The only thing was – what was one man against three desperate ones?

Sag-belly came lumbering to the door and told him to shut his face. What'n hell, did he want all the desert to know what they were doing?

Irons, out of the corner of his eyes, saw the prospector come running forward through the bushes – and saw the glint of light upon steel and guessed that he had a rifle in his hands. He also guessed that there was probably some gold around, because of the way that man came quickly forward. He came with a swift rush, like a man reckless to protect his property, and Irons didn't rate much for his chances, alone and in that incautious mood.

So he spurred his horse towards the door of the cabin, guiding it with the pressure of his knees. He shouted at the big fellow inside: 'I don't give a damn ef the desert does know there's three no-account, thievin' *hombres* tryin' ter steal a poor fellar's gold.' That told the advancing prospector what he was up against. It also brought Irons' horse right across the front of the cabin.

Sag-belly got worked up. 'Shut him up, Lem. Ef he opens his trap agen, beat him outa the saddle with your rifle butt. The hell, he'll have someone down on us, the way he's shoutin'!'

Lem snarled a threat and hoisted his gun significantly. But Irons was watching the fringe of bushes across from the cabin. He saw a movement – guessed that the prospector was halted back there, wondering how to tackle these men who were going through his property.

Irons, bound though he was, showed him the way. The moment he saw that glint of a rifle barrel again, he acted. His horse was suddenly startled – and pained – to get the mightiest kick in the ribs it had ever had. Iron Jack didn't like doing it; he loved horses and would never wear spurs or harm a beast if he could help it. But right now he felt that a kick in the ribs was something that could be forgiven, if it saved his life and helped the prospector. The horse whinnied and lashed out. And it was just as Irons had planned it. Those feet lashed out just when he'd manoeuvred the beast so that Lem was standing behind it. Lem shouted with pain as the hoofs kicked into his arms, sending the rifle high into the air.

Then Irons bounded away. He twisted in the saddle, shouted, ' Thar's a couple more in that cabin, fellar. Wing 'em as they come out.' And let his startled horse crash in among the bushes.

A shot rang out, and it came from the scrub. There was a howl of pain from sag-belly. Twisting, Irons saw the three former employees of his company all scrambling by the doorway. They'd tried to get to the other two horses, to mount and flee in panic at the thought that there was an armed enemy in the bushes. But that swift shot from the hidden prospector sent them scurrying back inside the cabin for cover.

Irons worked his way around in the scrub until he came up behind the prospector. He shouted because the hidden marksman couldn't be sure of him, of course.

'I'm cumin' up fer you to untie my hands, brother. These galoots had got me tied.'

A thin, yapping voice, that sounded old and dry and full of alkali. 'Yeah? Who're you? What do they want ter tie you up fer?'

Irons answered only one of the questions; he thought that would be sufficient. 'I'm Jack Irons, boss of the Pacific Coast section of the Pony Express—'

But he didn't need to say any more. Most men knew of Jack Irons in Nevada, and his reputation was sound, for all the talk of outlawry in Kansas. The desert rat barked: 'C'mon up, Mister Irons. I'll sure be glad ter help yer.'

Irons shouted: 'Watch out. Them fellars is slippery.' He didn't risk riding in on the horse, but somehow rolled himself off it. His wounded leg was so stiff that he could hardly bend it; all the same he managed to crawl up to where the dried up runt of a prospector was crouching.

Irons saw a wrinkled, wizened old face, then rolled over on to his side. A not-so-sharp knife blade hacked at his bonds, and then, glad moment, he was free!

He had to relax, just lying there and stretching and getting the movement back into his cramped arms, for several minutes. In that time he told the old timer what had befallen him.

The old man spat brown tobacco juice into the sandy soil. 'You done me a good turn, Mister Irons,' his thin, sharp voice quavered. 'Reckon that was mighty quick of you, way you got that warnin' ter me – an' then told me there was three fellars a-waitin' fer me. I got a bit of gold hid under that firestone at the back, an' I figger they'd sure have found it but for your help.'

Irons straightened. He was feeling better, and anxious to get going now. 'You don't need to thank me for anything. This makes the score even, brother,' he told him. Then he said: 'What are we gonna do about them birds?' He was thinking it was a waste of time handing them over to the sheriff of Virginia City.

The old man speculated. Probably he was thinking the same. Then he said: 'You goin' back to town?' Irons nodded, still rubbing the marks on his wrists. 'Mebbe you could call in at a li'l camp right across on the trailside. I've got a few friends there, prospectors like myself. Jes' tell 'em ole Mulehead's got a bead on some gold-minded gents, an' they'll come an' help me settle these varmints.'

Irons didn't ask him how they'd settle things. He wasn't interested. He just knelt and looked through the scrub. The other two horses had wandered off, looking for grazing; the men were trapped inside a cabin that had no windows and only the one door they were staring into.

If the men showed in the doorway, old Mulehead would drop them like sitting ducks – and they knew it. Irons could hear a murmur of conversation within the cabin. The three teamsters seemed in a panic, and they were arguing among themselves and blaming each other for this fatal halt at the prospector's cabin.

Irons said: 'So long,' and crawled back to the horse. It took him a lot of effort and a considerable amount of valuable time to get into the saddle, but at last he was up, and once there, like the true cowpuncher he'd been for so much of his life, there was no getting him out of his seat.

He rode hard southwards until he came out upon the rutted trail that scored the surface of the scrub desert. Turning west, within a couple of miles he rode on to a collection of miners' shacks, where about a dozen prospectors lived close together for protection.

Irons saw a short, bent man who either had a beard or he didn't shave more than once a month. Irons called down: 'Mulehead's in trouble. Go an' help him, will you?' The bent man looked at him, recognized him, probably, nodded and ran shouting in among the huts.

When Irons was less than fifty yards along the trail to Virginia City, he looked round and saw five men galloping into the scrub on bony desert ponies. He felt satisfied that justice would be done to the three men whose greed had got them into trouble.

He slept by the trailside that night, curled up in a bush that kept the slow, cold, night wind from him. He was so tired that he never woke once until a good hour after the sun had risen.

Again he could hardly move when he tried to go out to his patient, waiting horse, but after a few minutes the circulation came back to his limbs and he felt better than he had done for several days. Even his head wasn't aching this morning.

He had no food or drink, but got some and a Colt and ammunition from a solitary wagoner who was taking a load of nails on to Austin. The wagoner made a few remarks about his appearance, but Irons couldn't be concerned about such trifles. He was too anxious to get back to Virginia City to find out what had happened to Ann and his beloved Pony Express.

He was five miles from the town, at a point on the trail where a track led off to distant Crooked Ford, when he saw Shep Clayton come high-tailing it from Virginia City. Shep didn't recognize him at first, but when Irons shouted, the young trail boss whooped with delight.

They swopped talk quickly. 'Miss Caudry's fine,' Shep assured him. Then he went on— 'Look, Jack, Virginie City's stiff with Awker's men. We've got rumour that they're plannin' ter swipe the mail when it comes in, so Thompson said for me ter tell the Pony Express man to ride round the town. Tommy figgers on avoidin' any more trouble.'

Iron Jack's eyes were grim. 'I've had enough from Awker,' he growled. His face under that mask of dust lifted to Clayton's, and it was as hard as quartz. 'This time I want ter settle with him fer all time.'

Shep said: 'Sure, sure, boss,' not really under-standing, and Irons knew it. 'So?'

'So the mail rider's gonna ride into town after all.'

'What?' Shep was startled.

'Sure. I don't want a show-down averted. I want it ter happen now – today – on my terms.' His mind was racing, looking along that dusty trail that wound over the scrub mesquite to the distant Virginia City. 'Ef the Awker mob attack the mail, we've a right to defend it with all we've got. OK?'

'Sure, that's OK.' Then Shep pointed out: 'But, look, boss, we've got around twenty men sittin' in that town – twenty men an' a gal. And there's two hundred Awker men there ef there's a dozen. There isn't time ter get the men in from the camp. Mebbe a coupla dozen,' he admitted, remembering the newly arrived horses, 'but what's that agen Awker's hundreds?'

Irons said tersely it was suicide, then said: 'So that's why you're not goin' fer the men. They c'n stay out under the wagons an' rest. Instead . . .'

He spoke rapidly to Shep, at the end of which time his assistant seemed suddenly pleased and readily agreed to swop Irons' tired mount for his own comparatively fresh one.

Then Shep Clayton rode away, and he was heading for Virginia City, this time, leaving big Jack Irons to sit his horse on the trail.

# CHAPTER TEN

Iron Jack heard the swelling roar of men's rough-edged, triumphant voices. To the waiting Awker men, this was their moment – now they would get their revenge on the Kansas outfit for the drubbing they'd had two night ago, and even before that.

Suddenly those big, rough, hairy-chested teamsters were racing down the street, converging on the Pony Express office. Iron Jack saw them coming, and it was the moment he'd waited for. He'd wanted them to attack him – he'd wanted them to try to get the mail.

But they didn't get it. Iron Jack was too quick even for the nearest of the Awker men – those men who had been deputed to stand so close that they could intercept the mail carrier when he came off his horse. As he came out of the saddle, his arm swung and the light leather *mochila* with its four letter-pouches, the *cantinas*, went hurtling up the steps to where Thompson and his men were crowding at the open doorway.

Then Iron Jack wheeled, and those men who were about to jump him saw a Colt gun in his hand . . .

and their plans had been based on the theory that a Pony Express man never carried a weapon, because even such a small weight became a burden in that long race across the continent.

Iron Jack shouted: 'Stand back!' Then stood and faced the onrushing mob. When they saw that one resolute man facing them, they came to a sudden halt, a few yards away, standing momentarily like suspicious longhorns.

Then a roar of fury rose as the mob suddenly realized that once again they might be thwarted by this grim, travel-stained man they knew as Iron Jack.

They began to come on with a rush. Iron Jack retreated up the steps, flourishing his gun and holding back the leaders of the crowd. But the pressure of the mob behind forced them on towards him, and he gave way.

One of the men came down – an out-rider with his guns out. He stood alongside his boss as Iron Jack slowly limped backwards until they gained the door to the office. Then suddenly they stepped inside and the door was slammed in the face of their enemies.

And then the mob woke up to what had happened. Everything had occurred in a matter of seconds, and they were too slow-thinking to realize that from the first their plans had gone awry.

They'd been told to stand around and grab an unarmed man and run off with his mail – those two hundred teamsters were there to make sure there was no pursuit; they were going to block all roads out of town afterwards.

Only, they hadn't been able to lay hands on the mail. That quick throw had hurled it beyond their grasp. And that unexpected gun had balked them in any slow-developing plan to wreak vengeance upon the quick-witted man who had once again defeated them.

Inside, Thompson was shouting to men to get to the doors and windows, back and front. He knew there'd be a big fight now. Jack Irons stood in the passage, recovering his breath. Ann fought her way through the mass of men, all intent on getting to their positions, and fell into his arms.

'Oh, Jack,' she whispered. 'I thought I was never going to see you again!'

'And you wanted to – badly?' he found himself asking.

'You don't know how badly,' the girl told him, holding him, her head on his chest. She was near to weeping, he could see, and that made him uncomfortable – he didn't know how to handle weeping women.

So he put his arm across her shoulders to give himself support, limped in to where Thompson had a gun poking under the window in a side room where the jockeys slept. As they entered, the glass crashed above Thompson's gun, and lead smacked against the far wall.

The first shot had been fired in the battle of Virginia City.

All around the Pony Express office, irate men found positions behind barrels and corners of buildings and then opened up with every weapon they had. A shout had gone round from someone – perhaps from Awker himself in the background – that the mail wasn't going any further. It was going to be dragged out from that office – it certainly wasn't going to be carried on to the next stage.

And then someone had an idea. They began to hear it inside the building, above the crackle of gunfire.

'Smoke 'em out! That's the quickest way of dealin' with the mail!'

The shout became a roar. Inside the building the defenders, sniping back wherever they could, saw a fire buggy being prepared up the street. A cart was dragged out, and a lot of boxes and inflammable material was stacked on it. Then it was saturated with lamp oil, and then towed to a position on the slight slope until it was opposite the office.

The defenders saw the danger and smacked back with every weapon they had. The noise of battle was tremendous, inside that echoing wooden box of a building, and to make matters worse, the horses in the stable behind were terrified and were whinnying and kicking and threatening to crash the wall down on them.

Above the din Iron Jack's voice shouted: 'Hold 'em off! There's help comin'. Keep 'em back a few minutes more, that's all I ask!'

They didn't know where he could find help so magically at this moment, but they'd never known Jack Irons to let them down and they took heart and ripped off at their enemies so that they fell away from the fire buggy.

It began to roll. Just as it started on its slow journey towards the Pony Express office, someone hurled a bundle of blazing rags on to it. Instantly it became a raging fire – a moving thing that crept slowly but certainly down towards the tinder-dry wall of the building.

Thompson got to his feet, shouting: 'We can't stop in here, Jack. Everyone get out the back way. Take the hosses – fight your way out!' Though it didn't seem much of a prospect, fighting a way through a circle of savage besiegers.

But Jack Irons was shouting again, countermanding the order. 'Outside, everyone – the front way!' he roared. He was stooping at a window, peering beyond the blazing wagon. 'Outside an' stop that wagon hittin' the office. The Awker men won't hurt you now!'

It was as inspiring as a bugle cry, to hear that confident shout of triumph from their boss. When he led the way, they came out swiftly behind him.

And the Awker men never looked at them. For now the real battle of Virginia City had begun.

There were men pressing in from every side street, and their guns were blazing off at the Awker men. And these were tough, clay-begrimed miners, fresh in from the nearby diggings. Leading them was a middle-aged man – the man who had spoken to Jack Irons about cleaning out the Awker mob with a vigilante movement.

Thompson shouted in delight: 'You did this, Jack! You old son of a gun, you fixed things for the Awkers!'

And the Awker men were being well and truly fixed. There were hundreds of irate citizens of Virginia City, returned unexpectedly early from the diggings, incensed that their town should be used as a battlefield by the Awker outfit. They were tough men, hardy, as useful with a gun as with a pick. And now they came out and they gave the Awker crowd the biggest thrashing of their lives.

The battle swayed as men clashed; but there was never any doubt about the result. The Awker men were demoralised by the upsetting of what had seemed a cast-iron plan for revenge. And in their hearts they knew, too, that they were in the wrong, and they quailed before the fury of these vengeful citizens of Virginia City, who for too long had seen the outfit bully the town and hold it to ransom because of the monopoly on freight haulage.

Steadily they were beaten backwards, out from the centre of the town. Then the fighting continued down the side streets, and out on to the open land beyond, where the cast-up mounds of earth showed the beginnings of the diggings.

And then came a moment when they'd had enough. When they stopped resisting and simply turned and stumbled away, back to their gutted, burnt out camp.

A mightily pleased vigilante chief rode right out to Crooked Ford late that evening to tell them that the entire Awker outfit was pulling out, heading West. 'Reckon that bad-tempered li'l Awker fellar knows there ain't no future fer him in Virginie City no more. Reckon he's had enough thrashin's, this last day or so, an' he's pullin' up stakes an' gettin' ter hell outa Nevada.'

'Then all our troubles are over.' That was Thompson, pleased, because he didn't like trouble. He wanted things to run smoothly and without fuss. He'd been told how Jack Irons had swopped horses with the Pony Express rider when he came racing along the trail. Irons had come in with empty *cantinas* as a decoy, leaving the Pony Express jockey to cut round the town and make for the next way station in the Tahoe Hills. Virginia City mail could come back later.

And Shep Clayton had ridden to the diggings at Irons' order to find a vigilante chief and tell him. what the Awker crowd was planning. Anything against the Pony Express was felt by these miners to be something against themselves, and they had downed tools at the call of the vigilante chief for a show-down with the Awker mob.

Well, Thompson was thinking, they'd had their showdown. But he wanted to see the business running without showdowns, and at the news of the Awker outfit's trek from town, he let optimism blind him to reality.

But it didn't blind big Jack Irons – or Ann Caudry. Jack smiled down at the girl, but there was little humour in it.

'What do you think, Ann?' he asked softly.

And she told him: 'There'll be more trouble. Awker won't forget this defeat, and he's still powerful – very powerful at the Pacific end of the trail. We'll have another fight yet.' And then she added: 'Awker's bad medicine, but I fear Weyte more.'

Then she smiled up at him and hugged his arm. 'But, Jack, I'm beginning to think there's no one in the wide world who can defeat you. You're – you're marvellous, Jack.' Her eyes were shining.

He said, comfortably: 'There's the gal fer me. Jes' keep thinkin' like that. I like it.'